Fiona McDonald

GREEN LANDS

When Nancy took a position as secretary to a powerful businessman, she soon found herself in dangerous waters

WITH *DANCING IN THE WINGS* - A BALLET STORY

Mereo Books

2nd Floor, 6-8 Dyer Street, Cirencester, Gloucestershire, GL7 2PF
An imprint of Memoirs Books. www.mereobooks.com
and www.memoirsbooks.co.uk

GREENLANDS
ISBN: 978-1-86151-889-7

First published in Great Britain in 2021
by Mereo Books, an imprint of Memoirs Books.

Copyright ©2021

The address for Memoirs Books can be found at www.mereobooks.com

Mereo Books Ltd. Reg. No. 12157152

Typeset in 10/17pt Plantin by Wiltshire Associates.
Printed and bound in Great Britain

Prologue

Nancy Lockhart was born in South Africa in the year 1952, the daughter of David and Margaret Cummings. The Cummings had lived in Forres, Morayshire, before venturing in the 1940s to South Africa, where they had a vineyard. Nancy's grandparents, Anthony and Mary Cummings stayed in Forres.

Nancy attended Forres Academy, staying with her grandparents, but spent her holidays in South Africa. After the deaths of her grandparents, her parents returned to Scotland.

Nancy had the qualities to be a Secretary and worked in London at an insurance Company. She met Christopher Lockhart at a dance; he was an engineer. They fell in love and got married. The marriage was a happy one, but unfortunately she could not have children due to Christopher contracting mumps as a child. Then, after twenty years of marriage, Christopher passed away with a fatal heart attack.

Years later Nancy's father died too, which left her mother, Margaret, sad and lonely. Margaret Cummings had been a strong woman; she had held authority while living in South Africa. She dominated her husband and fellow workers, who were afraid of her. After her husband passed away she became a recluse, hardly venturing out, and developed dementia. She depended on her daughter to look after her, but sadly she began to lose her memory, and Nancy thought it was best to place her in a home where she would be looked after.

This story begins in the year 1999, when Nancy, who is living in Edinburgh, applies for the post of secretary to a land developer.

Chapter 1

The train pulled into the station at North Berwick, East Lothian, and Nancy Lockhart stepped onto the platform. She was to be met by one of Gordon Mackenzie's employees, who would take her to the house for her interview. She had answered an advertisement for a secretary.

Nancy was tall and good looking, with brown hair and blue eyes. She was dressed in a lilac costume and black shoes, and carried a light black jacket. She walked towards a black car, where a man was leaning against the driver's door. It had been quite a long time since she had had a full time job, but after her husband had passed away, she worked temporarily. Life was not easy with her mother now living in a nursing home.

The man leaning against the car was smoking a cigarette; he looked up as she approached him and threw it away.

"Are you Mrs Lockhart?" he asked.

"Yes I am, and you are?" she said, coming up to him.

"Joe." He opened the car door. She entered the vehicle, and placed her bag and portfolio beside her.

After a short drive, the car turned into a long driveway and approached a large white house standing in its own grounds. There were gardens to the left of the house with flowers and plants, which gave off wonderful aromas. A glass building was attached to the house; it looked as if it housed a swimming pool.

Nancy was ushered into a small living room with a large television in the corner. There were bright rosy curtains which hung down to the floor, and small window which looked out at the garden. She sat on a sofa, and glanced through her portfolio. She was aware that somebody had entered the room, and as she stood up her portfolio fell to the ground.

"I am Gordon Mackenzie, and you will be Mrs Lockhart, I presume?" he said, smiling. "Welcome to Greenlands." He motioned her to sit down facing him, and handed her the portfolio.

Nancy suddenly felt nervous, and dug her nails into the palms of her hands. Mr Mackenzie interviewed Nancy, and she told him of her past experiences in secretarial work, with something of her life in South Africa. When the interview came to an end, they went upstairs to a large lounge where they had coffee. The house was situated between a small village called Macmerry and North Berwick, East Lothian, and had good views towards the Fife and the Firth of Forth.

Mr Mackenzie showed her around the house. There was indeed a swimming pool, but Mr Mackenzie told her he did not use it, except for the grandchildren.

Nancy noticed that he was having had a good look at her, his eyes inspecting her from head to toe. She wondered if he was looking for a wife, or perhaps he was lonely.

Her suspicions were confirmed when he invited her to dinner at the Marine Hotel in North Berwick; they set off in his sports car. During dinner, he offered the post to her, but Nancy asked if he would put the offer in writing. She did not want to appear too keen, but the salary and the work sounded interesting, and the hours suited her.

It was late when Nancy returned to her flat in Bruntsfield, an area of Edinburgh. She lay on the couch, listening to the news, but not really taking in what was being said. She thought of her interview that day, and the enjoyable dinner they had had in North Berwick. Mr Mackenzie seemed to be charming, but she wondered how many secretaries had been in his employment. Who else worked for him, she wondered? He had mentioned two men who worked in an annexe, and were out of the office.

A letter finally arrived, confirming the arrangements for her employment and informing her that a Ford Fiesta car was to be picked up at a garage in Sighthill, Edinburgh, for her use.

After a fortnight, Nancy took up the post. The work

was mostly typing up reports and attending meetings at Greenlands or in Edinburgh. She was introduced to the two other employees. Sam Wilkinson was born in London, single and in his late thirties. He was tall with black hair and brown eyes and had trained as a financial advisor. Joe Higgins was born in Edinburgh, had attended Boroughmuir School, and had trained as a draughtsman.

Nancy did not have much to do with the two men, as they worked in a separate building. She did find Sam was very polite, but Joe gave her some very odd looks. Gordon Mackenzie did not seem to mind or notice these incidents, but he was rather bitter about his ex-wife appearing at the office.

Nancy still had to meet the rest of the family, including Gordon's sisters, his daughter and grandchildren, who all sounded very spoilt.

Nancy was kept busy. Gordon held a lot of his meetings at the house or in Edinburgh, but the meetings in Edinburgh were longer, as there was quite a lot of travelling to do.

Gordon was so different from Nancy's husband; he seemed to be shy, quiet at times, but he had a sense of humour. He also had a temper, which one saw at meetings when things were not going his way. The men at these meetings smiled at her, and wondered how on earth she put up with such a bad-tempered person. But he always apologised to her, as he knew his behaviour was wrong. She could not really argue as he was her boss; she just had to put up with his moods.

Gordon found Nancy to be a first-class secretary who always had the work up to date. After working for him for a few weeks, she started to notice that he was becoming rather friendly, asking her out on several occasions to dine with him. He knew, of course, that she had an elderly mother living in a nursing home, and sometimes at weekends it was not possible for Nancy to socialise. He also noticed that she did not seem to have any friends who asked her out, although she was a good-looking woman. He had had a few lady friends since his divorce, but nobody special, and now he was looking at Nancy in a romantic way.

Nancy was not sure about Gordon. She enjoyed going out on social occasions, but all the attention scared her. She found working at Greenlands quite creepy. There was something about it which she felt was not quite right. She preferred it when Gordon stayed over in Edinburgh, especially if he was attending a concert or going to the theatre.

He hardly spoke about his family, but Nancy knew that one day she would have to meet his daughter and grandchildren. She also knew that the two sisters were married, one living in Haddington, East Lothian, and the other in Livingston, West Lothian. He hardly saw them, but he knew that they were curious to meet Nancy.

One day, the parents of the grandchildren turned up, and Gordon had to entertain them. His daughter, Lisa Johnston, was a tall woman with brown permed hair. Her husband, David Johnston, was around five feet ten, with longish hair.

They were introduced to Nancy and Lisa looked at her as if to say 'who the heck is she?' Nancy felt very uncomfortable, but she smiled and asked if they would like some coffee. David grunted, and they made themselves comfortable in the conservatory. Gordon came into the kitchen and started to apologise, but Nancy kept her mouth shut and did not say anything. She made the coffee, placed some biscuits on a tray and carried it through to the conservatory, placing it on a small coffee table.

Lisa seemed to be very nosey, and asked Nancy how long she had been working for her father. Nancy put the tray of cups down and poured out the coffee. "Four weeks," she said. She did not like the way Lisa was looking at her. She made an excuse, saying that she had work to be completed, as she felt the atmosphere was rather explosive.

Lisa and David usually dropped off the children and went shopping. The one person she had yet to meet was his ex-wife, Doris, but she would wait for Gordon to tell her about her in his own time.

Gordon took Nancy for a short holiday to a hotel in Benalmadena, in the Costa del Sol, Spain. Nancy made sure that they would be staying in separate bedrooms. They visited Rhonda, with its famous gorge, Mijas, where the views were magnificent, with donkey rides for children. Malaga had the Alhambra Palace, where the Moors had resided years ago. Time flew by, and they both enjoyed the holiday and had a good time.

The first time Gordon had suggested that Nancy should stay the night at Greenlands, she wondered if she should accept. After all, they were a courting couple. Gordon had a bedroom downstairs at the rear of the house and Nancy was relieved that it was not upstairs among the ghosts. This was the first time they made love.

On Nancy's return, she was informed that her mother's health had deteriorated. The matron of the home told her she had had a stroke. Nancy was really worried, and spent most of the following days by her mother's bedside. Gradually her mother's health improved.

Gordon knew his daughter Lisa was not amused by Nancy. She thought she was a stuck-up bitch who was probably out to trap her father into marriage.

Gordon had made a will, leaving his children land and property. He had come to love Nancy very much indeed; she had a lovely smile and a great sense of humour. Nancy was always ready to work and attend meetings, but she always insisted on returning home afterwards.

Gordon's two sisters, Jean and Ursula, turned up one day. Jean was sixty-six years of age, married to David Wallace, and lived in Livingston. They were not blessed with children. Ursula was sixty and married to William Donaldson. They had grown-up children living in Fife, but they had stayed in Haddington.

Nancy only met the sisters for a few minutes as she had work to finish for the next meeting. Nancy thought Ursula looked very like Gordon, with the same nose and eyes. Of course, they were interested in where she came from and where she had been educated. Nancy left that for Gordon to inform them.

Nancy did not like staying over at Gordon's as she found the house rather chilly and not at all welcoming. This was not the house Gordon and his wife had lived in when they were married, but Gordon liked his home, and was happy working there.

Joe did mention that Greenlands was haunted, and she wondered if that was true or if he was just trying to frighten her.

Gordon and Nancy went out most Sundays for a long drive into the countryside, which helped her to relax after the strain of working and visiting her mother. Gordon never came to visit her mother, as he thought it was best not to, and he felt Nancy did not encourage him to visit. He knew she was tired, and told her to take some days or a week off to deal with urgent matters at her home.

One day, Ursula turned up for afternoon tea. She was a tall woman with blue rinsed hair and long fingernails painted bright red. She was dressed in a dark suit with a large brooch pinned on her jacket. She sat on the chair with one leg over the other and sipped her tea with a finger pointing upwards, smiling at Gordon.

Of course, she was delighted that her brother had found someone. She really wanted to know how his business was coming along, but Gordon would only tell her what he wanted her to hear.

"How is the new secretary getting on?" she asked, gazing over her teacup at him.

"She the best one I've ever had, I cannot fault her work at all. She is also very good looking and very charming," he said, knowing his sister was very curious.

"She comes from South Africa, or she was born there, and her parents are Scottish and from up north" she said, giving him a smile.

"Yes, she was born out there, but she was educated in Moray Academy up north," he said, not going into too much detail about Nancy.

"You know dear, you should find yourself a nice lady friend," she remarked, raising an eyebrow at him.

"Have you and Jean been scheming to find me a wife? I am happy at the moment and have too much work to think about without chasing women," he said, getting up and placing his cup on the tray. He was hinting that she should leave. She got up and kissed her brother on the cheek, squeezing his arm.

Gordon showed his sister to the door and waved goodbye as she got into her car to drive away. He breathed a sigh of relief and took the tray and placed them in the kitchen sink before going to the conservatory to smoke a cigar.

Chapter 2

It was nearly Christmas, and Nancy had brought in some presents and cards to the home so that her mother could give presents to the friends she had made there. She had made friends with a woman who had been a matron of a hospital and was very fond of crosswords, and together they used to do the puzzles together. She had also made friends with a woman who used to walk outside on the pavement with her two sticks to get some exercise. The others, in her mother's eyes, were not right in the head, as her mother put it, and she could not have a conversation with them. Her mother did not know about Gordon, and Nancy had never mentioned him, just to keep her mother's outlook right.

Her mother passed away on the 20th December, 1999 at ten-thirty in the evening. The matron of the home had phoned Nancy to inform her that her mother had deteriorated that day. Nancy felt glad in a way, because she knew her mother suffered towards the end, and yet she had lost a mother and a friend. She informed the matron of the home that she would come in the next day and collect her mother's belongings, so that the body could be taken to the undertakers and the room made available for the next patient.

Nancy was busy arranging the funeral, which would now take place after the New Year, as everything would be closed over the festive period. She was an only child with no brother or sisters, so she felt alone. There were cousins who lived on Jersey on the Channel Islands, but Nancy was never in contact with them.

Time had to be taken at the funeral parlour looking through brochures for the right kind of coffin, flowers and wreaths, and Nancy felt quite exhausted. However, Gordon phoned and made arrangements to take her out to lunch to cheer her up.

Over lunch she looked pale and tired, and played with her food without really enjoying it. Gordon was talking, but her mind seemed to wander about. Should she contact the cousins after all this time, or should she just leave it? How many people would turn up? Her mother had stipulated that she wanted a private funeral, and to have her remains put in the garden of remembrance, which would save her money instead of going up to Forres, where her father was buried, and anyway there was probably no room in the burial plot, as the grandparents were buried there.

Gordon placed his hand over hers and smiled. "I know

how you are feeling my dear. I am here to help you, you are exhausted trying to do so much by yourself, please let me help you take some of the burden."

Nancy smiled, trying to keep the tears back. She placed her hand on his.

"I know you're helping me, and I am so grateful to you for taking me out for lunch to cheer me up, but to be honest, I could do with a rest. I want to celebrate Christmas and the New Year with you and your family."

"What you need, my dear, is complete rest. I am sure everything is now arranged for the funeral. I'll take you home and give you time to recover. When you're ready, please get in touch with me." He pushed back his chair and helped Nancy to put her coat on.

Nancy was grateful that Gordon understood, as she knew that she would not be very good company at the present time. She lay crying in bed before drifting into a deep sleep, but this made her feel even worse when she woke up.

Christmas came, and it was spent quietly at Gordon's. He took her out for Christmas lunch at a hotel in North Berwick, and afterwards his sisters turned up with various presents. The evening became quite jolly for Nancy, and she joined in the conversation and games. She was glad his daughter did not turn up.

The weather was cold and frosty, especially in the early mornings. Nancy, who was still staying at Gordon's, took a stroll amongst the flowers. Breakfast was a modest meal, as Gordon was not a big eater, and he only normally had cereal in the mornings. Nancy took cereal or porridge and toast. Of course, when she was working the breakfast was smaller, due to the working day. As she did not want to stay at Gordon's for too long, she made sure she went home to Edinburgh. She was invited for New Year celebration at Gordon's.

At New Year's Eve they went for dinner at a hotel, and then came home and opened a bottle of champagne to toast in the New Year. Nancy felt a bit tipsy, and Gordon was in a great mood, as he was slightly drunk. They put on some music and danced before retiring.

The sales were on in Edinburgh, and Nancy and Gordon went into town for some shopping. Nancy did not know what she wanted, but ended up getting an overcoat, which Gordon insisted on buying for her. He was not much of a shopper, but he knew what he wanted and went for it. The crowds, however, soon became unbearable.

Back home, Lisa and David turned up uninvited with the two children. Nancy and Gordon were sipping tea in the conservatory when they arrived. The children shyly stared at Nancy, but gave Gordon a big hug and a kiss. Nancy smiled.

"We came to wish you a happy New Year for 2000. We should have phoned but we knew you would be in, you usually are," said Lisa to her the father. She ignored Nancy.

Gordon stood with one of the children hanging onto his arm and nagging at him.

"We were having some tea and were about to go out, but since you have arrived, I'll make a fresh pot of tea with some sponge cake," he said. "Off you two go and tell me if the cats need feeding." He pushed the children out of the back door, then went to the kitchen to boil up some more water.

Nancy was left standing facing Lisa. David grunted a Happy New Year to Nancy, and sat down in the corner looking out of the window. There was silence for a moment, and then Nancy broke the ice by asking if they had had a good Christmas and New Year.

Lisa looked at her painted nails before replying. "Oh, we were in Spain over the festive season, and had a wonderful time, much better than this country where it rains and is so awfully cold."

Just then Gordon appeared with the tea and cake. The children dug their fingers into the cake.

"Hey, not so fast, go and wash your hands," Gordon said, handing out napkins and plates.

The tea party was a bit of a strain, and Nancy was relieved when the family decided to go home. Lisa had ignored Nancy, talking to her father the whole time, and David had looked at his fingers the whole afternoon.

Chapter 3

Nancy lay in bed looking up at the ceiling. She had a nasty cold and was not feeling well, so she had insisted that she should stay at home and rest. Her throat was sore and her nose was red from wiping it so much. Gordon had insisted that he could stay with her, but when she was not feeling well, she would rather be by herself. She knew he would keep coming in giving her drinks when all she needed was to sleep.

She dreamt of her youth in South Africa, where her father had vineyards. The house was built with bricks, with long steps leading up to the front door and a veranda on each side of the door. There were outhouses for the workers the men and women needed at harvest time.

When she woke up she glanced at the clock, as Gordon had mentioned that he would phone at 5 pm. She swung her legs off the bed and slowly sat up, placing her hand over her brow. She felt awful, and staggered into the kitchen to put the kettle on for a hot drink.

She found some Lemsip sachets in a packet, and placed one in a mug, pouring the hot water into it. Then she stirred it and took a sip moving towards the lounge and the couch. She switched the television on, and pulled her dressing gown around her.

The phone rang, making her jump; she stood up and went towards the small table in the corner and picked up the receiver.

"Hello dear, how are your today?" asked Gordon.

She sneezed, then raised her hand to her brow. "I'm not feeling too good, and I think I must have a cold or flu. I feel awful and maybe running a temperature. How are you coping over there?"

"Fine, but I really do miss you; perhaps I could come over and look after you," he said.

Nancy could not face him or anybody. "Don't come over, I don't want to give you the flu, I'll be all right. I'll phone you tomorrow." She sneezed again.

For the next few days Gordon did not know what to do. He sat down and put the television on with a glass of whisky and started to think. Why was it his daughter did not like Nancy? Obviously she was jealous. Of course, Lisa had airs and graces above herself; in one word, she was a snob. She had been sent to a good school, so there was no excuse for her behaviour. God only knew why she had married David, who was a good joiner, but useless in company, as he hardly said a word.

After a week Nancy returned to work, much to Gordon's pleasure, as he had several meetings to attend to and wanted her to be with him. Lisa's name was not mentioned, although he had spoken to his daughter, and told her to grow up and behave herself in company. He had fallen in love with Nancy. He had known he would ever since she had come for the interview that afternoon.

Nancy had now worked for six weeks. She knew he was busy, and the work seemed to get busier, with more meetings. He would be working over the weekend, until she had suggested going away then to do some shopping in Glasgow, see a show or concert, and return fresh to start work on the Monday. He seemed to be agreeable to this suggestion, as he had noticed that she was becoming rather moody.

She wondered if she would ever return to South Africa; perhaps it was past history. Gordon would not like the hot weather, so it would have to be in spring or autumn.

She wondered, if Christopher had lived, if she would have accepted the post at Gordon's. Although all through her married life she had worked full time, she had found at times that it was hard work, especially for a housewife.

She thought of Sam and Joe. She really liked Sam, but Joe had a mean streak about him. He was always staring at her, which made her feel uncomfortable, and she tried to avoid him if he came into the office.

She found when staying at Gordon's that she heard creaks and other noises coming from upstairs. She made a point not to investigate the upper floor of the house, and wondered if someone else was staying there or whether it was a ghost. She always meant to mention this to Gordon, which made her somewhat afraid. She knew that Gordon wanted her to stay at his house, as she knew he was lonely and enjoyed her company.

One day, she went to the stationery cupboard to get some printing paper. As she opened the door to place her hand on the light switch, she felt something brush her arm. She yelled and something moved past her. She turned around to find one of the cats running out the door.

Joe had come in and stood looking at her laughing his head off. She was annoyed that he was finding the episode so funny. She put the light on in the cupboard and reached for the paper she needed, then said to him, "So glad you find it so amusing. I just had the fright of my life." He stood trying to keep his face straight looking at her.

"No ghosts, or did you think there was one in the cupboard?" he said. She closed the cupboard door and said to him "Very funny". She walked past him and made her way back to her room, and he followed, still laughing.

"Here, this parcel arrived this morning, could you give it to Gordon?" he said, lifting his hand to cover his mouth as he was still laughing. She looked at him. How dare he laugh at her? Her heart was still thumping from the fright the cat had given her. She took the parcel he handed her, and he went off, still laughing.

Chapter 4

A friend called Jennifer came to stay for a weekend at Nancy's. It was nice to have female company for a change. Jennifer had been at school with Nancy, but now lived down in York. She was divorced, and her children were grown up and married. She was tall with mousey brown hair, brown eyes and spoke with a slight lisp. She had a great sense of humour, and laughed at her own jokes.

"So you have been working for six weeks for Gordon Mackenzie," she said. "What's he like, handsome?"

Nancy laughed. "Well, he's tall, has grey hair, a nice smile, quite serious at times, and I think he is in love with me."

Jennifer raised her eyebrows, "Wow. Are you in love with him? Do you think he will ask you to marry him?"

Nancy looked at the friend. She had thought about marriage, She was fond of Gordon, but she was not in love with him. The work was good, also the wages. She enjoyed the meetings with other men, whom she sometimes flirted with.

On Saturday, Nancy and Jennifer went shopping in Princes Street, did some sightseeing, and returned quite exhausted. Nancy cooked a meal, and they talked about old times. There was a ring at the door, and Nancy went to see who it was, as she was not expecting anyone.

Gordon stood at the door with a bouquet of flowers. Nancy was surprised to see him.

"Oh hello, come in" she said, opening the door further and stepping back. She wondered what he wanted. "I have a friend staying with me over the weekend. Let me introduce you. Gordon, this is Jennifer, an old school friend."

Jennifer stood up and shook hands with Gordon. Nancy noticed that he was having a good look at her.

"Nice to meet you" said Jennifer, sitting down on the couch. She looked over at Nancy and raised an eyebrow. Nancy took the flowers from Gordon and went into the kitchen to find a vase. Gordon followed her. "I thought you were alone, I would have phoned, but I was in town so I took a chance to drop in and see you" he said, feeling rather embarrassed.

"Would you like a drink? Wine, whisky or something?" asked Nancy, opening a cupboard to get some crisps and place them in a bowl.

"I'll take a small glass of whisky with some water" said

Gordon, opening the bottle and poured some liquid into the glass. He followed Nancy back into the lounge.

They made small talk, and eventually Gordon left, feeling he was intruding. He had really wanted to find Nancy alone. He had been thinking about her. He really wanted to ask her if she felt the same way as he did, as he was going to ask her to marry him. His sisters were asking about their relationship.

Nancy and Gordon went to a meeting in Moray Place, Edinburgh, where a firm of builders was hoping to buy land to build houses. A tall man with fair hair and blue eyes called Bob Jones stood up to give his talk. He had been sitting beside Nancy, and gave her a smile. She smiled back and thought how handsome he was. The whole time during his talk he looked at Nancy, and she hoped Gordon had not noticed.

Gordon refused all the offers which were given at the meeting, as he thought they were all far too low. Nancy had the job of writing to each one of them.

A few days later Nancy began to feel unwell; she told Gordon that it had started after the coffee, when his family had come round to visit. Lisa had insisted in making it, as Nancy was busy in the office typing documents. She had to get these documents finished for a big meeting in Edinburgh that afternoon. She had her coffee at her desk. She put her hand up to her forehead, and felt quite sick. She was ill in the toilet, and felt hot and sweaty. What was wrong? She had felt fine that morning. She returned to her desk, and took a drink of water.

The family left at lunchtime, and Nancy managed to eat a small amount of cheese and biscuits, with some weak tea. She felt better after being out in the fresh air, and let Gordon drive to their next meeting, also about selling land to house builders, and she remembered the last meeting she had had a month ago. Unfortunately, Bob Jones he was not at this meeting. Gordon argued about prices, and she knew in the end that he would not give in to their offers. She wondered how he ever did business at all. She would be typing the refusal letters.

Finally Gordon did accept an offer from Taylor Woodrow, who were interested in some land between North Berwick and Haddington. He was quite excited at the prospect of receiving some money, and immediately got Nancy to type out forms and agreements. But it had been a long day and she had had a dreadful morning with Lisa, with the children all screaming by the swimming pool, so she insisted in returning to her flat in Edinburgh. She wondered why Lisa had wanted to make the coffee instead of Gordon, who was busy looking at papers. He was not amused that the family had turned up on a work day, as he had no time to really entertain them. Of course, that was typical of Lisa. She probably knew that Nancy would be there, but why insist on making the coffee?

Suddenly it occurred to Nancy that she was the only one not feeling well, as Gordon seemed to be perfectly all right. Had something been put in her coffee? She started to wonder if she was being poisoned.

She told Gordon that she had been feeling unwell after the coffee, but he told her it was probably something she had eaten at breakfast time. She asked him. "Why weren't you feeling unwell?" He just shrugged and told her not to worry.

Gordon phoned Lisa and told her not to come in on working days, as he was too busy with important issues. Lisa told him she would only come at weekends. Gordon told her that he and Nancy usually went away to relax and get away from work at weekends, and he did not want anyone in the house. She remarked, "You never used to be like this, you welcomed your family with open arms, but since you met that woman, you've changed. Why did you not stay with mother? Are you going to marry this woman?"

Gordon began to lose his temper; he knew that Lisa was a strong-willed lass. He replied, "Don't speak to me like that, this woman has a name and it's Nancy. I want you to be polite to her and respect her. You know your mother and I never got on, and it was best we divorced; we never should have got married." He banged the phone down, leaving Lisa seething with rage.

Nancy was glad to return to her own home. It had been hard to concentrate with the children running in and out of the house. She always felt uncomfortable at Greenlands, and asked him again what the creaks were upstairs. He told her that it was an old house, so it must be the heating system.

One day she did venture upstairs, just out of curiosity, to find out what was up there. She knew there was a large lounge on the first floor, but where did the other rooms lead to?

She moved towards the first door on the landing and was about to turn the handle when suddenly there was a loud bang like a door being closed, and she panicked and flew down the stairs.

Chapter 5

Two weeks later Gordon was invited to a business dinner in Edinburgh, and he invited Nancy to accompany him. It was a formal do, and Nancy was quite glad to get dressed up for it. Businessmen and women usually attended these functions, but on this occasion friends were invited.

Nancy dressed in a blue velvet outfit, one her mother had made up for her some years ago. They got a taxi to the Conference Centre in Edinburgh, and made their way to the large reception area, where a glass of champagne was handed out. Nancy was rather apprehensive at being there, as she knew she did not know too many people. Gordon was well received, and he introduced her as his secretary.

The dining area was packed with tables spread out around the room, and Nancy and Gordon were placed with some businessmen she had met at meetings. The meal was three courses, with various choices for starters and the main course. Nancy took melon cocktail to begin with, and then roast beef with vegetables and for her sweet she chose vanilla ice cream with hot apple pie. Every one spoke at once, and the wine flowed, with the conversation mainly about planning or land development, which Nancy found rather boring.

She looked around at the other tables, and caught the eye of a gentleman who looked familiar, but she could not place him. He smiled at her and lifted his glass in acknowledgement. She smiled back at him.

After dinner everyone seemed to stand around with drinks in their hands and talked in groups. Nancy made her way to a side table, which was filled with after-dinner mints. She noticed someone standing beside her, and as she picked up some mints, he spoke to her.

"Long time since I last saw you. You were taking notes at the meeting I was at. I hope you remember."

She turned and looked straight into the eyes of Bob Jones. She found herself blushing. Of course she remembered him, as she had often thought about him. There was something about him that made her feel sexy. She found him exciting, and could not help staring at him.

"Of course, I remember you," she replied. "You did the speech regarding land development, and Gordon refused to take up everybody's proposals, I had the job of writing to all of you." She smiled.

She swallowed a mint, and began choking. She feared

she was making a fool of herself, and took the glass of champagne he handed her.

"Would you like to have lunch or dinner with me?" he asked. "I find you very interesting."

Nancy smiled and replied. "Yes, that would be very nice indeed. You know I still work for Gordon Mackenzie, but that's another story. I live in Edinburgh, Bruntsfield, do you know it?"

Bob sipped his champagne. "Yes, I know it. I live on the south side of Edinburgh and work in an office in George Street. Could you manage a day next week, or will you be too occupied?"

Nancy looked at him. Oh yes, she wanted to get to know this man; he was far more exciting than Gordon.

She opened her evening bag, but could not see any paper or a pen. He handed her a business card and a pen and she wrote down her number on the back of it.

The party was beginning to thin out, and she looked around to see if she could see Gordon. He was talking away to a group of men, looking rather drunk. He was always the last to leave. She moved towards the group.

"Here comes your secretary, Gordon," remarked a stout man, looking directly at Nancy.

Nancy looked at Gordon, who smiled at her and tried to put an arm around her. The men saw that she was going to have some difficulty in getting him home.

"Best get him into a taxi and home, he's drunk a bit too

much champagne," said a slim man, holding on to Gordon's arm. Nancy looked around to see if she could see Bob, but he had left. She smiled at the men, and one of them said he would get a taxi, and moved off to the reception area.

In the taxi, Gordon was talking a lot of nonsense, telling her how much he loved her. She felt quite exhausted. When they got to the house she managed to get him on to the sofa in the lounge, where he fell asleep. Nancy made herself a cup of tea, and changed for bed. She looked into the lounge to see if Gordon was all right; he was sleeping. She slipped under the duvet on her bed and cuddled down, thinking about Mr Bob Jones. How good looking he was! She wondered if he was married. She had not noticed any rings on his fingers, and hoped he was not.

The next morning, she awoke to find Gordon standing beside her. He stood looking at her, and at first she blinked, as her thoughts and dreams were still with Bob Jones.

"Good morning my dear, you look beautiful," he said. She had never encouraged Gordon to hug or kiss her, as she did not want a close relationship with someone she worked for, so she got out of bed, pulling her dressing gown around her shoulders.

"I'll get some breakfast. Do you want a cooked breakfast, or a continental one?" she asked. "Looking at you, perhaps some coffee and toast." He looked as though he had a bad hangover.

"That would be good" he said, running his hand over his face. She turned away. But she was thankful it was a Saturday, and did not have to get up for work. Deep down, Nancy did not want Gordon to stay another night. However, after breakfast, he surprised her by putting his arms around her as she was doing the washing up and planted a kiss on her neck. She turned around and he kissed her hard on the lips, pulled her close to him intimately and whispered that the dishes could wait for later. Then he led Nancy through to the bedroom, where they made love.

Chapter 6

It was a week after the dinner in Edinburgh, and still Nancy had not heard from Bob. She sat at her desk looking out of the window, and wondered why she had been so hopeful about meeting him once again. Why had he not got in touch with her? She knew that she should not really think about him in a romantic way. What would he really be like. Certainly he would be more romantic than Gordon, who seemed to be so occupied with work that they hardly kissed or hugged.

Bob Jones sat at his desk and looked at the drawing he had done. It did not look right, so he tore it up and placed it in the waste paper basket. He looked at the phone, and knew that he should have contacted Nancy, but the week seemed to have flown by.

Bob was separated from his wife Rita, who had moved

down to London to work, as their marriage of three years had not worked out. They had no children, which was a blessing, and the separation was easy for both of them. The marriage had been rather stormy, as he was having various affairs, and in the end Rita had had enough and applied for a post down in London. They were still good friends, but living together had not worked out.

As Nancy opened the front door and placed her shopping in the hall, she heard the phone ringing. She picked it up, and was glad to hear Bob's voice. She had been beginning to think that he had forgotten her.

"Hello, am I speaking to Nancy?" Bob asked.

"Yes, that's right."

It's Bob Jones from the other week, remember?"

"Why hello there, how are you?" she said, delighted that he had telephoned her.

"I must apologise for not getting in touch with you, but work has been busy, and I've not had a moment, but I have been thinking of you," he said.

Nancy swallowed. Her heart was beating fast. "I've been busy as well, but we are beginning to see the light of day now," she said. Was he going to ask her out, or was he unsure?

"How about this Saturday evening? We could go for a meal, and see what happens."

"Yes that would be wonderful, where shall I meet you?"

"I'll meet you outside the Roxburgh Hotel at seven. Is

that okay? I won't take the car, as we both need to wind down and enjoy ourselves."

"Yes, that's great. I'll meet you at the hotel at seven pm," she said, sitting down.

"That's wonderful, I'm so looking forward to seeing you again. Bye." He rang off.

As Nancy sorted out her shopping in the kitchen she kept smiling to herself. Roll on Saturday! She would make an excuse to Gordon, just in case he wanted to come over. He always arranged something for the weekend, whether it was a show or a meal out somewhere, or just watching television. He enjoyed sports, and would sit for hours watching them.

It was late February, and the nights were cool and sometimes misty, but Nancy put on a warm blouse and skirt with a warm coat and boots. She was so looking forward to meeting Bob Jones.

She took a bus down to the west end of Edinburgh, and walked towards the hotel. She hoped he would be on time, as she hated waiting around outside shops or buildings.

He was there, standing tall and handsome. He came forward to greet her. He kissed her on the cheek and put his arm through hers.

They dined at an Italian restaurant in Hanover Street; it was very busy, being a Saturday evening. She told him all about her life in South Africa and London where she had met her husband, and how it had gone wrong, and she told him about Gordon.

They left the restaurant and went to a hotel on Princes Street for a quiet drink. Nancy was feeling relaxed and enjoying Bob's company. They took a taxi to Nancy's, where she opened a bottle of wine. As they talked Nancy again felt strongly attracted to this man; he was so handsome and had a generous mouth with nice eyes.

Bob looked at Nancy; he found her attractive, if not beautiful. She had a nice smile and kept her hands and nails manicured; today they were painted pink. He liked her a lot. She laughed and smiled at his jokes, and was good company. He wondered what she would be like in bed, and wondered if it was too soon for that. He was attracted to her, and if he played his cards right, he hoped he could win her affections.

Nancy gazed at him while he was speaking to her. She in turn was wondering what it would be like to go to bed with him. The thought of it made her feel quite randy.

It was getting late, and Bob finished his glass of wine. He was obviously going to kiss her, and if she responded to his kiss, then she knew the next date would be straight into bed to make love.

Bob gently bent down and brushed his lips against hers. He felt her press close to him as she returned his kiss. They stood together, the kiss getting deeper, until Bob hugged her and let go. He promised to be in touch, and with that he disappeared out of the door.

Nancy closed the door, leaning her back on it, and gazed

ahead, smiling to herself. Yes, he was so handsome, and she never felt this way with Gordon.

She went into the kitchen and poured herself another drink from the nearly empty bottle. How was she going to get through the week without being in touch with Bob? She downed her glass, placed everything in the dishwasher, turned off the light and made her way to the bedroom.

Bob got a taxi home, and when he arrived he threw off his coat and made straight to the drinks cabinet. He poured himself a whisky, added some water and sat down and gathered his thoughts on the evening with Nancy. Why was she not married? Of course, she had been widowed some time ago. She certainly seemed to like him, and he liked her a lot. He was separated from his wife and they were not in touch, so he might as well enjoy life. He downed his drink and made his way to the bedroom. Yes, he was definitely going to keep in touch with Nancy.

Nancy was relieved to learn that Gordon had to go and visit his daughter in Edinburgh that weekend, as one of the grandchildren was ill. The little lie she had told Gordon about being ill had turned out well. Of course, he was now worried about her, and wondered whether she was feeling all right. She had gone to work on the Monday with her thoughts on her meeting with Bob. Was she now falling in love with this man she had met only twice before?

Bob could not help smiling over his mug of coffee at his work as he thought about Nancy. He had not felt this excited for quite some time, and was looking forward to asking her out again, knowing that quite possibly they would end up in bed making love. The very thought of it made him hard, and he slipped his hand down over his crotch and squeezed his balls. He looked around to see if anyone had noticed, but they were all busy working.

Nancy and Gordon had another meeting in Edinburgh with Taylor Woodrow, and it was decided that Woodrow was to go ahead and apply for planning permission to build on the land they had bought from Gordon. Gordon was happy, as he knew the cheque would be coming his way, and money would appear in the bank. Nancy returned to Gordon's, where she typed up another agreement to be sent for signature.

Gordon suggested that they should go out for dinner that evening, so they went to the Marine Hotel in North Berwick. He also suggested that she stay the night, which Nancy had not thought about. She felt more comfortable back home, knowing that a phone call from Bob could happen very soon. However, rather than having to explain herself with an excuse, she gave in.

When they returned they found Gordon's sister and her husband standing at the door.

"Hi! We dropped in to pay you a visit, but if it isn't an appropriate time we'll go," said Ursula.

Gordon sighed. He did not really want to entertain his sister, but rather than being rude he invited them in. He opened a bottle of champagne, and told them he had made a successful deal with a building company. Ursula was delighted. She jumped up and gave her brother a big hug.

Nancy sat quietly and let them talk away, as she did not really know his sister and husband all that well. She answered their questions. Ursula spoke to her, knowing that Nancy was very curious about her.

After they had left, Nancy washed the glasses, as they could not be put into the dishwasher. She hoped Gordon would be fast asleep when she entered the bedroom. She was definitely a night person and not a morning person, but she knew that Gordon was better in the mornings, as he often fell asleep in the evenings.

She took her time in the bathroom taking off her makeup; she had left several belongings at Gordon's, including clothes and makeup. When she was ready she tiptoed into the bedroom, and was glad to see that he was asleep. She lifted up the covers and slipped in beside him.

He opened his eyes, and smiled at her. He said. "Oh my dear, I do love you so very much" and he bent his head down and kissed her on the lips.

Nancy closed her eyes. She smiled at him and said, "You must be tired after the meetings and greeting your sister, I know I'm tired."

Gordon looked at her, and gave her a hug. He said. "You know my dear, you're right, I am tired. It has been a long day. Perhaps we should try and get some sleep." He gave her a good night kiss, turned over and went to sleep. Nancy was relieved; she did not want to make love to Gordon.

Nancy lay back and thought of Bob Jones. She would ask him to dinner, and see what happened afterwards. Was she falling in love with him? He made her feel so sexy. She would have to wait and see what happened.

On the Thursday evening Bob phoned, delighted that she had invited him for a meal at her flat. He would turn up at 7pm on the Saturday. He was looking forward to seeing her again, and kept remembering how she had pushed her body against his as he kissed her good night. He would buy some flowers and bring a bottle of wine; that would relax them both, and set the mood.

That Saturday Gordon was invited to his sister Jean Wallace's house for dinner, and most of the family were also invited. Jean was rather prudish in her views regarding unmarried couples, so she never invited Nancy. Gordon apologised to Nancy, and said that there would be a next time. She could go out with a girlfriend to the theatre, or a film, and hoped that she would enjoy herself.

Nancy was relieved, as she was beginning to run out of excuses. She got the meal ready and changed into a purple dress, low cut in the front, showing a bit of her bosom. She smiled as she glanced at herself in the mirror. She was rather nervous at seeing Bob again, so she had a small glass of sherry just to calm her nerves.

Bob arrived on time grinning from ear to ear, and placed a kiss on her cheek. She took the flowers from him and put them in vase, while he put the wine in the fridge. Then he grabbed her around the waist and pulled her close to him.

"You know I've been looking forward to seeing you again, and I've been thinking about you all week," he said. "You are lovely."

Nancy felt rather shy, but she smiled at him. She was not used to this sort of treatment, as Gordon was so conservative in his ways.

"I was looking forward to seeing you too," she said. "I feel a bit nervous." She turned to lower the gas under the potatoes, but he kissed her on the lips, drawing her closer to him. She tilted her head back, closing her eyes, and pressed against him. Her heart was beating fast; she felt this could go on forever.

After the meal and wine, Nancy put on some music, and they danced around the lounge with Bob holding her close. Nancy felt relaxed and rather merry, and she started to giggle. She kicked off her shoes, still holding on to Bob. After the music had stopped, not that Bob or Nancy realised that it had, they made their way to the bedroom.

Bob was undressed before Nancy, and into the bed. He watched her undress and slowly reached out, placing his hands on her breasts. He kissed them both in turn and smiled at her. She lay back looking up at him and then placed her arms around his neck, drawing him down so that he was lying on top of her.

They made love two or three times that night, and each time Nancy had an orgasm. This never happened with Gordon, and she wondered if it would always be the same when Bob made love to her.

In the morning, not too early, she made breakfast. She scrambled some eggs and fried bacon and tomatoes while making tea and coffee. He still looked handsome in the morning, and she wondered what he thought of her without make-up. She need not have worried. He smiled at her, holding her hand at the table. "This has been wonderful" he said, giving her hand a squeeze. "You are so loving and adorable,"

Of course, she was flattered, but then she thought perhaps he said that to all the women he made love to. She began to panic, and pulled her hand away, pretending to tidy her hair.

He helped her clear up, and even suggested that they could go back to bed and start all over again.

Nancy felt happy, and started the new week at work with a song that she could not get out of her head. Gordon noticed, and asked her how she had enjoyed her weekend. She said she had enjoyed herself and had gone out for a meal with a few girlfriends which had lasted the whole evening. God, all the lies she was telling him, and he believed her. If she was going to have an affair with Bob Jones, how on earth was she going to cope? She knew she could not keep up with two relationships.

Doris, Gordon's ex-wife, turned up one day at the office, and asked to speak to Joe Higgins. Nancy was busy typing away. She looked up at the small woman with dyed blonde hair, made-up eyes showing black eyeliner and blue eye shadow. Doris stared at Nancy, taking out a cigarette and putting it to her lips. Nancy rose from her seat and came towards her.

"He's over in the annexe working," she said. "Mr Mackenzie is in the Conservatory." Doris looked her up and down and replied. "You must be Nancy, Gordon's new secretary; he got rid of at least two that I know of." Nancy could tell that she did not care for her, but she smiled.

Doris shrugged and walked out. Nancy was glad to be rid of the rude woman; she could not blame Gordon for divorcing her.

Gordon returned with some more work for her to type out, and she mentioned that a small woman had turned up looking for Joe, but had not given her name.

Gordon grunted. He knew who Nancy was referring to. "What does she want?" he said. "I told her never to come here, even if she wanted to speak to Joe. Damn the woman. Sorry, that was my ex-wife, Doris." He looked very annoyed.

"No harm done, she left so she must have gone over to the other offices," said Nancy.

Nancy did not see Doris again, and she was glad to get on with the work that Gordon had given her to do. She wondered if Gordon had got engaged to his other secretaries, and when it did not work out they had left.

Doris had met Gordon at a students' party, held in a flat in Bread Street. They danced, and he saw her home to her flat in Leith. They became friends and eventually lovers before getting married, after dating for over eighteen months. Doris liked the good thing in life, and soon she became pregnant with Lisa. She bought lots of clothes through brochures, and worried about her figure. They were both unfaithful to each other and Gordon had had an affair, which had not lasted, and Doris demanded a divorce, although she also was having affairs. They tried to keep the marriage alive, but in the end it was best that they parted for Lisa's sake.

Doris was jealous of Gordon. He had made himself a wealthy and successful businessman, while she was inclined to be lazy, doing nothing to improve herself by studying.

Gordon lit up a cigar and glanced out of the window. The two cats were sunning themselves on the garden wall, and everything seemed so peaceful. He reached over and flicked his cigar into the nearest ash tray, and thought about his relationship with Nancy. She was so different from the other women he had dated; he had never got engaged to them. She was an attractive woman, proud in a way, perhaps because she was not Scottish, and maybe people who lived abroad had a different outlook in life. He had found that she was a very good worker.

It was getting late, and he wandered into the office, where Nancy was just finishing typing up the last of the reports. She looked up as he stood in the doorway.

"Time to finish, leave that, come and have a drink, it's getting late," Gordon said.

Nancy stopped typing; she placed the cover over the computer, and came towards him.

"That's all the reports completed for your meeting tomorrow," she said, letting him hug her. He kissed her lightly on the lips, gazing into her eyes.

Nancy looked at him, but it was not as exciting as being in Bob's arms. She smiled. He took her hand and led her into the large lounge, where he pulled her down on the couch, and placing his arms around her gave her a long kiss. Nancy did not struggle, but she pulled away and pretended to brush her hair. She did not want to stay overnight again with Gordon; she wanted to go home, and was hoping that Bob would be in contact with her again.

Every time she stayed at Gordon's, she felt nervous and wondered if someone else was living in the house. She sipped her drink and stood up, telling him that she needed to go home. He stood up and was rather angry. He gripped her arm and pulled her close to him.

"My dear, you are always rushing home, why not stay here for the night?" he said, trying to kiss her.

"No, Gordon I, need to go home, because I must have some time on my own, and besides I need to be away from the work atmosphere," she said, putting on her coat. She could not stay and have to pretend that she enjoyed his lovemaking when she knew she did not. He followed her out of the house and watched her walk towards her car. He stood in the doorway looking quite dejected.

"I'll see you tomorrow," she said. She closed the car door, started the engine, turned the car round and accelerated away. She hoped that Joe and Doris were not looking out of the window, as gossip would be spread among the workers very quickly.

Chapter 7

The following weekend David's birthday party was held at Gordon's with all of the family invited. Nancy was also invited, and she wondered how she could get out of it, as she wanted to be with Bob. She telephoned him and explained the situation, but he told her to go to the party, saying he would see her during the week. Bob was so understanding, unless, of course, he was seeing someone else. She knew she had to stay over at Gordon's, so she brought a small case with some clothes and makeup.

She got there early and helped the caterer to lay food and drink in the upstairs lounge. She dreaded meeting Lisa again, as she had not seen her for a few weeks and the thought of it made her nervous.

Gordon was dressed in a kilt and looked very handsome. He hoped that Lisa would behave herself, and not get too drunk and disgrace herself in front of the family. His sisters and their husbands were coming, and he was happy that the whole family would be attending the party at his house.

He knocked on the bedroom door where Nancy was finishing dressing. She wore a cerise dress with a black belt and shoes. He came up to her and kissed her on the cheek.

"You look lovely, and I want you to be the hostess tonight, not my sisters' or Lisa," he said. Nancy looked at him and replied "If you wish me to play hostess tonight I'll do so, but I think Lisa should be the hostess, as it's her husband's birthday."

Gordon shook his head and said, "Oh my dear, this is our house, not Lisa's and if she is rude to you, I'll ask her to leave." Nancy smiled and took his arm and they made their way upstairs to where the party was in full swing.

Lisa was standing beside her husband, and she looked straight at Nancy, but moved away as Gordon approached David to congratulate him, and Nancy shook David's hand. She gazed around the room and wondered if this would be how life was if she was married to Gordon.

The music blared out with Elvis Presley singing "I ain't nothing but a hound dog." The youngsters were jiving away to the music, and Nancy found it hard to talk and had begun to feel unwell, so she moved away to the entrance. She slipped away and went downstairs to the bedroom, then made her way straight to the bathroom, where she was violently sick. Was she catching something, or was there something in the food that did not agree with her? She hoped she would not be missed.

Gordon danced with his daughter Lisa, doing a slow jive, and David sat in an armchair drinking his beer as if it was someone else's party. He liked to sit and watch others enjoying themselves; he was really not a sociable person, except for having a drink with the boys down at the local pub.

"Come on David, come and dance with your wife, I'm getting too old for this sort of dancing" said Gordon, turning Lisa under his arm. He glanced around and noticed that there was no sign of Nancy. Where was she, and why was she was not entertaining his family? He looked at his sister Ursula.

"Have you seen Nancy?" he asked. Ursula shook her head and said "No, she was here a minute ago, do you want me to find her?"

"I'll go and look for her," said Gordon. "It is best I go rather than you, my dear." He left the room and went downstairs.

Nancy looked at herself in the mirror. She looked pale and her makeup was smudged, so she pursed her lips and put some more lipstick on. She knew Gordon would have missed her by now, and would have sent out a search party to look for her.

A loud knock on the door made her jump, and she immediately sat once again on the toilet seat.

"Nancy are you in there, are you all right? What happened, are you ill?" asked Gordon.

"Is that you Gordon? I've been sick, and I feel dreadful" she said, standing behind the locked door.

"Please open the door my dear. I am so worried about you," He turned the door handle.

Nancy unlocked the door. Gordon immediately came in and at the sight of her looking rather bedraggled, took her in his arms and held her. "My dear, what has happened? You were enjoying yourself, and now look at the state of you!" He pulled back and looked straight at her. Nancy sniffed, and began to weep.

"I don't know what has happened," she said, "I suddenly felt ill, and had to run down the stairs to the bathroom. I'm going to lie down for a while and if I feel better I'll join the party upstairs." She made for the bedroom.

"God this is terrible, I'll have to tell them that you are suddenly unwell," said Gordon. "They will understand, I'm sure of that. Would you like someone to come and stay with you, perhaps one of my sisters?" He placed a blanket over her.

"No. I just want to rest, I'll be all right, I just need to sleep" she said, closing her eyes.

Gordon kissed her brow, and tiptoed out of the room. He went back upstairs, and nobody said a word.

The party finished at midnight. A mini bus had been ordered that was big enough for everyone. Gordon mentioned something about Nancy, and everyone hoped she would recover.

The next day Nancy felt better. She did not want Gordon to get the doctor, and did not want any fuss. She insisted that she should go home and recover in her own place, and return when she felt better. Gordon of course, protested that she should stay with him, and get better with him looking after her. But Nancy wanted to be home, in case Bob phoned. She missed him, and wanted to see him again. After the disastrous weekend with the party, Nancy was glad to get home to recover. She had told Gordon that she would return to work, after she had had a check up at the doctor's. At home, she phoned Bob, and hoped he would still be keen to see her. She was now feeling much better.

When Bob heard his phone ring he drank his coffee and threw the empty carton into the bin, then took his phone out of his pocket, smiling when he saw who had called him. "Hello Nancy, how are you, and did you enjoy the family party?" he asked.

"Yes and no. I wondered if I had eaten something or drunk something odd, as I was ill halfway through the party, and had to lie down," said Nancy, sitting down and stretching her legs out.

"That's bad news, sorry to hear that, I bet Mr Mackenzie was none too pleased that you suddenly became ill. Anyhow, how about meeting up and say go for a meal somewhere and then back to your place or my place for good cuddle? I think you need a lot of loving."

Nancy smiled. "I really would like that. Where shall we meet and what time?"

"Oh, say seven o'clock at the Balmoral Hotel, this Saturday night, if that's okay by you? You will probably have to make up an excuse for lover boy!"

Nancy laughed. "I am so looking forward to seeing you again, I missed you," she said, hoping she was not being too bold. "I'm looking forward to seeing you as well, and I really did miss you at the weekend. I'll see you on Saturday at seven, and don't worry, I'll find a good excuse for Gordon." She giggled into the phone. "Honey, get plenty of rest before I see you. Goodbye now."

Nancy got up and went into the kitchen and made herself a cup of tea, which she took to the bedroom. She put on the side light and lay down on the top cover, stretching out her legs, and thought about Bob. Would he still love her as he did before, or would he end the relationship? What was she going to do with Gordon? After all, she was working for him, and he would not take too kindly if she told him that she did not really love him. Then there was the spoilt daughter, who demanded everything, and was still rather hostile towards her. The feeling was mutual, for Nancy she did not like her at all. That poor husband of hers just took everything in his stride and never really lost his temper. He just sat back and smiled.

Nancy recovered quite quickly, perhaps because of her date with Bob. She was so looking forward to seeing him again. Gordon had been on the phone nearly every day, telling her how he missed her, and Lisa and the children had been up most days to see him. He told her he had been out most of the time to meetings with various building sites in and around East Lothian.

Nancy felt quite nervous about seeing Bob, but he was there standing outside the Balmoral Hotel waiting for her. He kissed her lightly on her lips and put her arm through his, smiling down at her.

She smiled shyly at him. "Where are we going, or is it a surprise?" she asked, looking directly at him.

"Where would you like to go? Would you like English, Chinese, Italian, or a steak?" he said as they walked up North Bridge. "I cook a great steak, if you want to come to my place, or perhaps you think that's too soon after two meetings?" He squeezed her arm.

Nancy was hungry; she did not really mind where she ate, so long as she was with Bob. She thought for a moment. She knew she would land back either at her place or his, and it would be an overnight stay. She had packed in her handbag some make up, but no overnight clothes. She would not need them anyway.

Bob suddenly pulled her into a shop doorway, placing his arms around her and kissing her hard on the lips. She responded right away, moving closer to him and closing her eyes.

"Hey, you look a little bit pale, are you all right?" he asked, holding her away from him.

"Never felt better in my life and I am really hungry," she said, laughing as she cuddled him.

They stopped outside Ciao Roma restaurant, and went in. They were placed in a corner away from the other tables, which suited both of them. Bob did most of the talking while they ate, while Nancy listened. He spoke about his work regarding a hotel which was going to be built on the south side of Edinburgh.

After the meal, they caught a taxi and went to Bob's apartment, which was off the Dalkeith road. He lived on the second floor.

Nancy walked through the hall into the lounge. She went straight to the window and looked out at the view, to the east one could just see Arthur's Seat, and the other side looked on to other houses.

He took her coat and threw it over a chair, and then went to the kitchen to the fridge to get a bottle of wine. "I hope you don't mind red, as that's all I've got in," he said, uncorking the bottle. She smiled at him and sat down on the settee, crossing her legs, then leaned back, gazing at him.

"This tastes delicious, it is so warm," she said, sipping her wine. He sat down, placing an arm around her shoulders, and held her. She placed her head on his shoulder and closed her eyes. She felt happy and relaxed.

Bob insisted that she should stay the night, not that Nancy put up any resistance, and they made their way to the bedroom. "I've changed the sheets and bedding, as I hoped you would come and stay" he said, pulling the blind down and drawing the curtains. "The bathroom is next door." He pulled back the bedclothes.

Nancy made her way to the bathroom, where she put on more lipstick and undid her dress, slipping out of it. She stood in front of the mirror in her slip, and wondered why she was doing this.

"Are you okay in there, need any help?" he shouted.

"I'm fine, won't be a minute" she said. She unlocked the bathroom door and returned to the bedroom, where she stood in her slip.

Bob was in bed already, and he lay back on the pillows looking at her. She looked lovely, and he immediately felt himself being aroused. She moved forward towards the bed, lifting up the bedclothes, and slipped in beside him. They made love several times that night, and finally both fell asleep in each other's arms.

Nancy was woken by the sun streaming into the bedroom. She opened her eyes, trying to work out where she was, and fell back, closing them again. Thank god it was Sunday, and there was no rush.

Bob came through with a mug of piping hot coffee and placed it beside her, leaning over to give her a good morning kiss. She looked over at him as he stood beside the bed, then slipped further down the bed, bringing the sheets up to her neck. She smiled at him, and told him she wanted to tell him a story. He sat down beside her on the bed.

"I'm all ears," he said.

She smiled at him, placing her hand on his arm. "Well, it was when I was fifteen back in South Africa on my father's vineyard," she began. "A young lad a bit older than me came to help at harvesting time. He was tall, fair and very good looking. We all had to work hard to get the grapes in, and I helped him with some others. We laughed and joked, and one day when everyone had moved ahead, he kissed me hard on the lips. His mouth tasted of wine. At first I was rather taken back, and I looked at him shyly. I was surprised, as that was the first time any boy had actually kissed me. Of course, I didn't mention this to my parents, although I think my father knew we were getting close, and warned me to be careful. I knew he meant that I was to be careful in case I became pregnant."

"Go on, this is getting interesting," said Bob. "But I wonder why you are telling me this story?"

Nancy looked at him. "Shh, this could be the interesting part. I let him feel my breasts. He became quite passionate, pulled down my trousers, and before I knew it he was in me, moving fast and furiously. He hurt me, but I wanted him to make love to me. I never said a word to my parents, and thought he would be on his way and forget me.

The following year he didn't come, although I questioned my father about him. I knew in my heart that this was my first love. I wanted to tell you that story, as I've never told anybody else – not even my husband knew about it."

She saw that Bob was grinning.

"Why are you smiling? I'm sorry, it's just that I needed to talk to someone, I hope you don't mind," she said. Bob pulled her close and kissed the top of her head. She cuddled close to him. She knew in her heart that she could never tell this story to Gordon.

It turned out a beautiful day, and Bob and Nancy went for a walk up to Arthur's Seat, which millions of years ago had been a volcano. The views were good, and they could see the coastline of the Firth of Forth, and also the Pentland Hills. She was glad of the fresh air and the closeness of Bob beside her.

She knew she had to return home, and hoped that Gordon had not been phoning her. She could not bear to spend another night at Gordon's home with those awful noises, and wondered if Joe was right that perhaps there was a ghost.

Chapter 8

Nancy arrived at Gordon's on Monday morning to find him tucked up in bed, looking pale and ill.

"What happened to you, you look awful?" she asked.

"I was at a family gathering last night and had some chicken curry, which obviously didn't agree with me" he said, wiping sweat off his face. "Sam rang the doctor, and I'm expecting him very soon. I'm not sure who will be on duty." He lay back on the pillows, looking sorry for himself.

Nancy stood in the middle of the floor. Should she stay or go home? There were reports to be typed.

Just then, there was a knock on the door and a small man appeared, peering over his glasses at Gordon. "Well now Mr Mackenzie what has happened to you?" he asked.

Gordon tried to sit up. "Oh Doctor Evans, thank god you have come, I feel dreadful. It's food poisoning. I think I got it from an awful meal I had yesterday evening. I've been sick most of the night."

"Now, just pull up your pyjama top, and I'll check your chest. I'll write out a prescription, and your wife can get it at the chemist immediately," said the doctor. He handed the prescription to Nancy and turned back to Gordon. "Stay in bed all day, and tomorrow you will have recovered, and you should be able to get back to work."

The doctor left. Sam knocked on the door and enquired if everything was all right. Nancy gave the prescription to him, as she had to complete the reports for tomorrow's meeting at Greenlands.

She made herself a cup of coffee and took it to her study, where she gazed out of the window at the garden. She smiled to herself. If she finished in time, she could go for a swim in the pool. She avoided going to see Gordon, as she wanted him to rest, and she did not wish to start running about fetching things and behaving like a nurse.

When she had finished her work, she went to the swimming pool, slipped off her clothes and put on her bathing costume, placing her clothes on a nearby chair. The water looked so inviting; she placed her toe to test the water, and found it was not too warm. The pool was not large; it was five feet deep at the deep end.

She let herself down the few steps, and swam out into the middle of the pool. She swam some lengths, then decided that she would get dressed and return home earlier.

She looked in at Gordon, who was fast asleep. She

tiptoed out of the room, gathering up her coat and car keys and made her way out to the courtyard.

Sam came out and asked how the patient was getting on. She told him he was sleeping, and as she was up to date with the work, she was going home. They said goodbye.

As she sat in her car ready to drive off, a car roared up the avenue and pulled up quickly at the offices. The car door opened and Doris got out and went inside. Nancy wondered what it was all about.

As she drove home she suddenly realised that a blue car had been staying behind her for some distance. Was she being followed? Could Gordon have got a detective spying on her, in case she had other men friends? Had he seen her with Bob? She began to panic. She could not ask him, but she could say that someone had followed her home and see what he said. She knew she was being unfaithful to Gordon, but she did not want to break off her relationship with Bob. She must try not to think of these awful thoughts, now that she was working, and the pay was good too.

Doris was sitting on the edge of Joe's desk, swinging her legs, She lit a cigarette.

"I see the bitch has left early, or did she have a fight with Gordon?" she said.

Joe took a cigarette out of his packet. "No, Gordon's ill in bed, Sam got the doctor just before she arrived, I know how you hate her, but she's a good worker, I'll say that for her." He blew out the smoke, tipping his head back and looking at Doris.

"Oh, for god's sake don't tell me you have fallen under her spell" said Doris, taking out a mirror and looking at herself.

Sam came into the room and nodded at both of them, then sat down at his desk. Doris came over to him and leaned forward, showing the cleavage displayed by her low-cut blouse. "I hear Gordon's unwell, and the woman has knocked off for the day. What are you up to these days?" Doris asked, letting the smoke from her cigarette rise to the ceiling.

"Well, we're busy with a heavy workload, and short staffed at times, but we are gradually getting there," Sam replied. "Anyway it's late, so I'm going home. See you tomorrow."

He lifted his coat, took his keys out of his pocket and went out. When he had gone, Doris went over to Joe. She pressed her body close to him, lifted her head and pressed her lips onto his mouth. He returned her kiss and pulled her close to him, stroking her back.

Gordon had awoken and heard a noise, so he slipped out of bed and went to look out at the offices. He saw Joe and Doris arm in arm walking towards her car; he already knew what those two were up to. But what the hell did she want up here, interfering during office hours?

He glanced at the clock on the wall, and realised that it

was six o'clock. He went back to bed and lay back, thinking of Nancy. She was a very good secretary; she always had the work up to date. Yet their love life had diminished, and he wondered why Nancy was happy to work for him but not to be his lover. He had seen a change in their friendship, and had begun to wonder if she had met someone else. It was not one of the men who worked for him, although Sam was single, and Joe was having an affair with Doris. Who could it be? It was probably his fault, for overloading her with work.

The blue car that had been following Nancy into the outskirts of Edinburgh had disappeared, to her relief. Who was following her? This had never happened before. Had Gordon been suspicious and got someone to follow her home, or perhaps to see if she was meeting someone?

She parked the car, and gazed around just in case someone else was following her. She was glad to get into her flat and kick off her shoes, placing her feet into her slippers.

She made a cup of tea, and was relieved that she was not spending the night at Gordon's. He always insisted that she stay over; perhaps he was lonely and needed company. The whole house seemed dark and menacing, and she was afraid that a ghost would appear. She thought she was being silly. Of course, there was no ghost, as Gordon would not have stayed there since his divorce. She could not blame Doris for not staying there. She had not seen Lisa since David's party and was glad that she had not appeared up at the house.

Chapter 9

Nancy jumped as the phone rang, then realised that she had fallen asleep with the empty glass in her hand. She placed it down carefully on the table and ran to the phone to answer before it stopped ringing.

"Hello?" she said. There was a pause before someone spoke.

"Is that you, Nancy?" It was Bob.

Nancy sighed; thank god it was Bob and not Gordon.

"Oh hello Bob, I fell asleep after a rather uneventful day at the office. Gordon was ill."

"I hope you're feeling okay after our weekend," said Bob. "I was phoning to ask you if you would like to join me at a cocktail party the office is holding this Friday evening at the Roxburghe Hotel at 6.30pm."

Nancy brushed her hand through her hair. "Is it a dressy affair or is it casual?" she asked.

"Dress code is smart, not evening gowns. Will you come with me?" He was hoping that she would say yes.

"Yes, that would be wonderful, but would it not be embarrassing for you to tell them who I am?" she asked.

"It's nothing to do with them. Anyway, I really am missing you; I did enjoy our weekend together. Never mind that Gordon bloke. He should take better care of you."

Nancy giggled and replied that she was looking forward to seeing him again.

When she had said goodbye to Bob, the phone went again. Was it him again, having forgotten to say something else?

"Hello," Nancy said.

"Hello, my darling," said Gordon. "How are you now? I noticed that you were in rather a hurry in leaving."

Nancy sighed. What did he want?

"Oh, hello Gordon. I had finished all the reports, and it was getting late so I thought I had better return home before the rush hour. Was there something I had forgotten?" She was praying that he would not ask her out on Friday.

"No my dear, but I thought you could have stayed over to have a light supper with me. You're always rushing home these days. It's not as if your mother is still alive. I miss your company," he said.

Nancy closed her eyes, wondering what excuse she could give this time.

"It's only the beginning of the working week Gordon, and anyway your grandchildren and your daughter were supposed to be visiting you sometime today. Had you forgotten?" She crossed her fingers, hoping he would not ask her over to entertain them.

"Oh yes, of course, I'd forgotten. Perhaps I should write engagements down in a diary. I'll see you tomorrow my dear." He was cursing the fact that he had forgotten that Lisa was coming with the children to swim in the pool.

Nancy put the receiver down, and went to the kitchen to see what she could have to eat. She did not really want to spend the whole day and evening with Gordon, because half the time he fell asleep, and she was left looking at the television.

The next day Gordon felt a lot better, and he hugged Nancy as she came through the door.

"My, you look a lot better. How are you feeling?" she asked, throwing her coat over a chair.

"Oh my dear, it is so good to see you again, I missed you so much," said Gordon. He followed her to the kitchen and stood watching her fill the kettle.

"We'll have coffee in the conservatory, it's much brighter there" she said, placing the coffees on a tray and taking it to the conservatory. Gordon sat opposite her, and thought this was how it would be if they were married.

Nancy crossed her legs and looked at him. He certainly looked rather pale, and she wondered if she should take the meeting on her own.

"I had a swim yesterday in the pool, it wasn't too warm, but I enjoyed it," she said. He seemed very quiet this morning. She continued, "When I was driving home yesterday, I noticed a blue car following me into Edinburgh. I don't think that it has happened before. Do you know anything about this?"

Gordon sat looking at her. "No, I've no idea who that can be," he said.

Just then, two cars arrived and parked in the driveway, Three men got out and made their way to the house. They were obviously the men from Persimmon Homes.

The meeting was a rowdy one, with Gordon raising his voice a few times. Nancy tried to calm him, placing her hand on his arm. She realised that he was not going to give in to their demands, and in the end he got up and went out of the room. Nancy smiled and told them he had not been well. She suggested that perhaps they could continue the meeting another time. A date two weeks hence was agreed, after which the men departed.

Gordon had disappeared, and she thought that perhaps he had gone out. She placed the files from the meeting on the table beside her. She looked out of the window and noticed that Joe was approaching the house. She wondered what he wanted.

He opened the door, slamming it behind him, and stood in the doorway.

"If you're looking for Gordon, I don't know where he is" she said, looking at him.

"Oh, well you will do" he said, looking directly at her. This made her feel quite uncomfortable. She sat looking at him wondering why he had come over, as usually the men never came to the house. "The contract we are working on has a problem," he said. "If you see him could you tell him to come over to the offices?"

"I'll tell him if I see him before I go home," she replied.

He stood there looking at her and made no attempt to move away. She felt uneasy as he was looking at her as if he was undressing her.

"Is there anything else I can help you with?" she said, gazing at him. He shuffled his feet and said. "No, I don't think so. Sam will be at the office until six o'clock, so Gordon can talk to him about the wee problem we are having." He turned and walked out of the room.

Nancy shivered; she did not like Joe as he was always leering at her, which made her a bit afraid of him.

Gordon suddenly appeared. She knew that he had not gone out, as the car was still in the driveway.

"Oh Nancy you are still here. Would you like a cup of tea? I fell asleep in the conservatory and forgot the time," he said.

"Joe came over as they have a problem with a contract,

and he wondered if you could pop over and talk to them" she said, smiling at him. She did not really want a cup of tea, as she knew she would be going home quite soon.

"Come and have some tea, and then I'll go over and see what Joe and Sam want" he said, leaving the room. She got up and followed him into the kitchen. They had tea, with Nancy drinking as fast as she could, as she did not want to stay over and stay the night in his house. Gordon did not mention supper or inviting her to stay the night, and she was relieved. She said, "Joe's always looking at me. Sometimes it makes me feel uncomfortable."

"Joe likes the ladies, that's his trouble. He's probably hoping you would go out with him."

She looked at him. She could not believe what Gordon was telling her. She certainly did not fancy Joe,

"Well thanks for telling me," she said. "Did he ever take out your previous secretaries?"

"No, I don't think so" said Gordon, finishing his tea. "Don't worry about him my dear, you have me to look after you and take you out."

Nancy suddenly thought that maybe it was Joe who had followed her in the blue car.

Gordon left for the other offices, and Nancy looked to see if there was a blue car in the driveway.

Chapter 10

When Nancy arrived at the Roxburgh Hotel for the cocktail party, she made her way downstairs to the ladies' to touch up her makeup before meeting Bob. There were several women in the room all gazing into the mirrors and doing their hair. No one paid attention to Nancy as she listened to their babble.

Bob stood at reception with his hands in his pockets waiting for Nancy to appear. He had noticed that she was a bit pale these days, and wondered if Gordon was working her too hard. He did not really like the man; he was rather pompous and bad tempered, and hardly seemed God's gift to women. He was sure Nancy was a good worker, but she needed a lot of loving care, and Gordon was not the man to give that to her.

Nancy appeared looking very glamorous in a cerise dress, with a black wrap around her shoulders. She smiled at him, and he gave her a peck on the cheek. She looked lovely.

The waitresses were scurrying around the room with trays of drinks and canapés. Nancy put her arm through Bob's, and was introduced to various people. They probably wondered if she was Bob's latest girlfriend. Bob looked at Nancy; he knew that on Monday everyone would want to know who she was.

The party was only from 6.30 pm to 8 pm and most folk disappeared after 7.30. They were leaving the hotel when Nancy came face to face with Mr Turnbull from Taylor Wimpey. He seemed surprised to see her with Bob and not Gordon. He raised his eyebrows and smiled at her.

"Why hello Mrs Lockhart, so nice to see you again" he said, looking rather amused. Nancy was taken aback at seeing him, and in a panic wondered if he would get in touch with Gordon to report that Nancy had been with another man. Bob squeezed her arm and shook Turnbull's hand.

"I'm Bob Jones, a friend of Nancy's," he said. Turnbull shook Nancy's hand and gazed at her. She was looking lovely tonight; he clearly thought Bob was a very lucky man.

Outside, Bob hailed a taxi and they made their way back to Nancy's flat. When they arrived she changed her dress into something more comfortable, as she knew Bob wanted to make love to her. She poured some drinks, and sat beside him on the couch.

"That was a really lovely party, thank you for asking me to it" said Nancy, sipping her drink.

"Come here you gorgeous creature, you were the belle of the party. I was so proud of you. You're a very attractive woman" replied Bob, pulling her towards him and kissing her. Nancy lay in his arms, closing her eyes. She felt really happy. She was so contented being with Bob; maybe it was because he treated her as a lover more than a friend. She was definitely in love with him.

Bob and Nancy made love that evening, and Bob stayed the night. The next day they drove down to the borders, stopping at Galashiels, Kelso, and returning for a late supper in Edinburgh.

Nancy thought she should tell Bob about the little incidents at work, She began, "It was some time ago, as I was busy typing up reports for a meeting in Edinburgh, Lisa turned up and insisted on making the coffee. Sometime later on, I was violently ill and asked Gordon how was he feeling after the coffee. He said he was fine, and suggested that it was something I had eaten at breakfast." She paused.

"Go on, this sounds interesting," said Bob.

"Well it was at David's party at Gordon's – remember, I could not be with you that weekend. I was feeling good, but when the party was in full swing, I suddenly felt unwell and once again I was ill. Thinking back, I had been talking to Ursula, one of Gordon's sisters, and I had placed my drink on a table behind me. Lisa had been hovering around that area and I honestly think she put something into my glass."

Bob placed an arm around her. "To me it looks as if

Lisa doesn't like you, and obviously she's jealous of you. She doesn't like you being secretary to her father, and she wants to get rid of you. So maybe you're right about her, as you have mentioned that you don't like her either. But you have to have proof that she is putting poisons in your drinks. Does she come often to see her father? The best thing for you is to keep an eye out if she visits, and try and make the coffees or drinks yourself. I certainly don't want to lose you. Nancy, I do love you."

Nancy was so relieved that Bob understood what she had been saying; she kissed him, putting her arms around his neck. She felt safe around him, and wished she was working for him instead of Gordon Mackenzie.

Nancy spent the whole weekend with Bob, and was sorry that Monday was approaching quickly.

She arrived early at Gordon's. There was no sign of him, so she went to her room and started working. There was a meeting in Edinburgh at 2.30 pm, and she started typing out the documents. Sam appeared and wished her a good morning, telling her that Gordon had driven out to see some architects regarding some plans for future housing.

Nancy smiled at Sam. "How are you getting on over there in your offices?" she asked.

Sam shrugged. "Fine, Joe should be finishing off the project we are working on, and then on to the next."

Nancy liked Sam as he was a quiet chap and a good

worker who did not say a lot; perhaps he was shy. He left the room and Nancy got on with her work.

It was quite late when Gordon appeared, peeping around the door to wish her a good morning. Nancy smiled at him and said. "Morning Gordon, hope you are well? I've typed up the documents for the meeting in Edinburgh."

He nodded and left the room, making his way into the kitchen to make a coffee. Five minutes later he appeared with two coffees in his hand, and told Nancy to come to the conservatory. They sat opposite each other, and Nancy felt the atmosphere was rather cool. Was he speaking to her, or was he sulking?

She said to him. "Did you have a good weekend?" She drank from her cup. She felt nervous and wondered if Turnbull had told Gordon he met her at a cocktail party in Edinburgh on Friday.

"I want to speak to you Nancy," he said. "You see, I feel I have not been honest with you. I rushed you into a relationship, which I should not have done, because you are my secretary. You are a wonderful lady, a good worker, have everything up to date, I cannot fault you. I would like you to keep working for me, and I hope we will still be friends."

Nancy could not believe what she was hearing. She replied. "Gordon, I am fond of you, I do enjoy working for you. The reason you rushed me into a relationship was so we could have sex."

Gordon raised his eyebrows in amazement. "Well my

dear that is partly true, as I've never met such a glamorous woman before. I liked you the moment I saw you. You never complained about the work, or thought it was boring or too demanding. I know some of my family have been hostile towards you. Lisa had ample opportunity to educate herself, and make herself a responsible adult, but she has taken after her mother, who liked to daydream. Her husband David is another kettle of fish. He's quiet and watchful, never says much, but I am sure he knows that Lisa is jealous of you. Please don't worry yourself about my family." He smiled at her. Nancy was amazed at what Gordon was telling her, but she still felt she was working for the oddest family she had ever come across.

She had been offered jobs with several companies, but she felt that at the moment it was not time to change career. She was sorry for Gordon, as he was a quiet, shy man, not outgoing like Lisa.

Gordon did not say much on the way to Edinburgh, and Nancy kept silent, hoping that at this meeting he would not lose his temper and embarrass her. She knew that the men who came to the meetings felt sorry for her. The meeting went all right, and Nancy made the excuse that she had a headache, and would be returning home.

Chapter 11

The days dragged by, and Nancy was becoming bored. The work had become rather monotonous with the same routine involving meetings in Edinburgh and at Greenlands. Perhaps she needed a holiday; the last one had been long ago in Spain. Gordon did not seem to want to go anywhere, and she wondered if Bob would go with her somewhere nice. Bob had not suggested any holidays; they just met up for dinners and lovemaking.

Lisa and her children came frequently to the house to swim, and Nancy made sure that she was working there, and not near the swimming pool. Lisa continued to make sly remarks to Gordon about her. She wondered if Gordon took sides, and was inclined to take his daughter's point of view rather than hers. Gordon always relaxed when he was not working, and was as nice as pie to her. She thought about giving in her notice, but the wages were so good that she probably would not get the salary anywhere else that Gordon was paying her.

One day she went for a drive, not knowing where she was going. She wanted to get away and think. She loved Bob with his jokes and tender lovemaking, and wished that her relationship with Gordon was the same. Gordon still hugged and kissed her, but he knew that making love was something she did not want to do.

As she drove inland towards Pencaitland, she suddenly noticed that a Land Rover was driving very close behind her. She pressed her foot on the accelerator to go faster, but the Land Rover did the same. Whoever it was had no intention of passing her. The faster she went, the faster the other car went.

She began to feel uneasy, and turned down a side road, hoping that whoever it was would drive on. The Land Rover did the same, and she started to panic. It kept driving up to her bumper, as if it was going to crash in to her and then backed off. Whoever it was must be trying to frighten her. She swerved around the next corner knowing she was going too fast, and drove off into a field. The Land Rover kept coming, and then all of a sudden it drove off.

She sat for a while trying to breathe. Who was this person, and why were they trying to frighten her? Had Gordon decided to arrange this little episode, or did Lisa arrange it?

She reversed out of the field and made her way to Haddington, where she stopped at a coffee shop to recover.

She managed to sit by a window. Her hands were shaking as she held the coffee cup; she looked around the room, where women sat talking to their friends.

After a while she began to feel calmer. She had nearly finished her drink when Jean Wallace came into the room; she looked around and noticed Nancy sitting in the corner. She came over and sat opposite her.

"Why my dear, are you all right?" she said. "You look so pale." Nancy put her cup down and tried to smile. "Yes, I'm all right, just a bit tired, that's all." She did not want to go into details regarding the morning's episode. She wondered how close Jean was to Gordon, as they seemed a close family.

"My brother is obviously working you too hard my dear," Jean went on. "He should take you away on a long holiday. Of course, he was always a book worm, and mother had a dreadful time to get him to do some exercise." She ordered some green tea and fussed about with her gloves and coat. "I was just passing and thought I'd come in here for some refreshment" said Nancy, trying to make conversation. "I never really come to Haddington, it's a quaint little place."

"Yes my dear, it's very historical you know, St Mary's Cathedral is a famous church, we often go there on a Sunday. Do you and Gordon go to church? No, as Gordon is not all that religious. Never was, poor fellow. I suppose it was because he was the only man, with two sisters who spoiled him. He was very clever you know, had good marks in all his exams, and did well at university. Why he went into land and property... well who knows." She glanced at Nancy. "Are you interested in history my dear?"

"Yes I am. I was good at that subject when I was in school up north. My parents came from Forres in Morayshire, as did my grandparents. My mother died some years ago. I never had any brothers or sisters." She looked at Jean, who smiled over her cup, placing it down in the saucer. She patted Nancy's hand.

"Never mind my dear, you have done wonders with Gordon. He is a happy man, and loves you dearly." She put on her coat and stood up. "I must dash now as I've been visiting my sister, who has not been well. Perhaps we can do this again sometime soon. Look after yourself my dear." She walked out of the shop.

Nancy sat for a while. She felt she did not want to return to work, so she strolled around the shops before getting into the car and driving back.

When she arrived back at Gordon's, Sam came out to speak to her. She wondered if she had been missed. "Hello, Gordon was looking for you," he said. "He wants you to type some documents for a meeting. Are you all right, you look rather pale?"

Nancy swallowed. "I am fine thanks," she said. She headed off towards the house, not looking forward to meeting Gordon or his family. She found Gordon in the conservatory looking at some papers, and he looked up as she appeared. "Why my dear, where have you been?" he said. "I was getting worried."

Nancy sat down and looked at him. She really wanted to go home. She said to him, "I was not feeling too well, and needed to get some air, so I drove to Haddington. Jean turned up at the coffee shop and we had a chat."

"My sister? What on earth was she doing there? Perhaps visiting Ursula. You know they are very close and they always got on even when they were children. Now my dear, could you possibly type out this schedule for me, as it is urgent." He rose from his chair, handing her the document.

Nancy went to her room, sat down and began typing. She paused for a moment, looking out of the window, Lisa and family had left, and Joe and Sam were getting into a car and driving off. They were lucky to be getting away from the house, and probably going home.

Gordon entered the room, and told her when she had finished to come to the conservatory for some tea. She nodded, acknowledging him.

Gordon never really questioned her about her drive or her disappearance, but made small talk. He asked her to stay over and have some supper with him. Nancy paused before replying.

"Do you mind if I go home, as I am not feeling very well," she said. "I should be all right tomorrow."

Gordon looked at her. She was always making some excuse. Perhaps she was dating someone, and wanted to be there in case he phoned or appeared at her home. She did look rather pale, but then it could be women trouble. He said. "Of course, you can go home my dear, and I hope you will feel better tomorrow."

Nancy was relieved. She gathered up her belongings and stood up.

"I'm sure I'll feel better, I know we have another meeting here tomorrow afternoon. Goodbye Gordon, see you tomorrow."

Gordon watched her from the door as she made her way down the long driveway.

Nancy tried to keep calm and not cry, but the morning's little episode had frightened her. She phoned Bob as soon as she got home. Thankfully he answered straight away.

"I've had a bit of a fright," she said.

"Are you all right? Perhaps I should come over and you can tell me all about it. You sound upset," he said.

"Yes please do. I'll make up some supper for us. I do hope you are hungry?"

"Yes, I'll be there in an hour and I'll look forward to seeing you."

Nancy went to the kitchen and opened cupboards, fetching plates and cutlery, laying the table and putting some vegetables and potatoes into two saucepans. She had some meat left from a meal she had had the other evening, and she placed it into a pan and made up some gravy to go with it. Then she changed into a dress, putting her feet into her slippers. She found some wine, and placed it into the fridge.

The doorbell went and she checked in the mirror, making sure she was presentable.

Bob came in and took her in his arms and hugged her. "You do look rather pale. Has something happened?" he asked, holding her hands and looking at her.

"I'm all right now that you're here. I always feel safe with you around," she said, hugging him.

Over the meal she told him what had happened that morning, and how Gordon had not seemed at all interested in what she had to say. "He's always complaining that I never stay over and have supper with him," she said. "I always feel I want to be home."

Bob took her hands in his and squeezed them tight. "It looks like Lisa arranged it, just to give you a fright, and there could be more episodes happening in the near future. Why don't you leave if you are unhappy?"

"I feel I can't at the moment, the salary is so good. Gordon is always trying to get me into bed, and I don't want to. What shall I do? I'm a wreck and worry too much." She suddenly burst into tears. Bob took her in his arms and caressed her. He kissed the top of her head, then turned her face towards him and planted a kiss on her lips.

"Oh my dear, I've never met anyone like you before. You are so delicate and so loving. Look, this is what you must do. Go in tomorrow as if nothing has happened, but be careful, trust no one, not even the blokes who work for him. You did mention that one of the lads was seeing his ex-wife. She could be encouraging the daughter to taunt you and scare you, so you'll feel vulnerable and afraid. In the end you'll leave, and she'll be back in with Gordon and become his wife once again."

"Oh do you think so? I could look for another post. Mr Roberts from Persimmon Homes offered me a job as his secretary. I've been tempted to take it. Oh Bob, I am so sorry to drag you here to listen to my complaints."

"Look honey, if you're upset it was right to call me, otherwise you will make yourself ill." he replied.

"OK. Will I see you this weekend? I promise I'll be a good girl and not moan about work."

"Come to my place and I'll cook you a gorgeous meal. I guarantee you will not be talking about Gordon or his family. I must be going, it's getting late."

He kissed and hugged her close, and promised to phone her about Saturday. After he left, Nancy felt a lot better. She went to bed, trying not to think about tomorrow.

In her sleep she dreamt that Joe had come into the room, and stood there with a smirk on his face, he said nothing, just gazed at her. She sat looking at him and wondered what he wanted.

"Can I help you?" she asked, hoping that he would go away. He smiled and came forward and stood with his arms folded staring at her. He said "Yes, I want you and I fancy you. Gordon can't have all the fun. I know you're dying for me to kiss you."

She laughed nervously. "You must be joking. If you were the last man on earth I wouldn't kiss you."

He immediately came up to her and kissed her hard on the lips, grabbing her by the shoulders. She raised her hand and slapped him hard on the face. That was when she woke and sat up wondering where she was. Thank god it had all been a dream.

Chapter 12

Nancy arrived at work later than she had intended, and wondered how she was going to face Gordon. She hoped the meeting was going to go smoothly without any hitches. She looked into the conservatory, but Gordon was not there, nor the kitchen or lounge. She went to her room and started typing documents that were already laid on her desk.

There was a knock on the door and Sam entered the room. He stood for a moment before speaking.

"Morning Nancy, just to tell you that Gordon's at the doctor's this morning, and he'll be in later on."

Nancy smiled at Sam. "I'll type up this correspondence as we have a meeting this afternoon. How are you getting on over there in the office?" She was glad that Sam had come over instead of Joe. She knew Joe did not like her, and wondered if it was he who had followed her yesterday.

"I hope you're feeling better this morning, you looked very pale yesterday," he said.

He wondered if she was really happy working for Gordon. She always appeared to be a good and efficient worker, but she was quiet at times. "I'm feeling much better now," she said "Thanks for coming over and the telling me about Gordon." Sam left and she carried on working.

Gordon appeared some time later on, and had brought some sandwiches for a quick lunch before the meeting. They had some tea in the conservatory as the meeting was at 2 pm. He was quiet and did not say much, and she did not enquire how he had got on at the doctor's. She made small talk during lunch, and told him that the documents were ready for signing at the meeting.

"You're a gem Nancy," he said. "You always have everything up to date. I can't fault you or your work. We should go out more together, because I do think you need to have some fun. We used to have fun when you first started here some months ago, but work has taken over."

Nancy smiled at him and nodded in agreement. She thought she could go out with Gordon during the week and Bob at the weekends. She started to get the room ready for the meeting, as time was marching on.

Four men turned up for the meeting and made themselves comfortable around the table. Gordon seemed to be in a good mood, and documents were signed for the next phase of building. After the meeting Mr Turnbull from Taylor Wimpey spoke to Nancy, saying he knew she was a good worker. He never mentioned meeting her at the cocktail party some time ago, and she was glad of that.

"Gordon seems to be in a good mood these days," he said. "I've noticed that you're very happy to work for him. I don't know what he pays you, but my dear I could double it if you came to work for me."

He smiled at her, waiting to see what she would say. Nancy gathered up the folders and thought for a moment. It was so tempting to leave Gordon and his family, but what was the salary Turnbull was offering?

She smiled at him. "Mr Turnbull, I am rather taken aback at your offer. I would need to think about it. It depends on what salary you would be offering me. Mr Mackenzie's salary is pretty good, more than you'd even get down south."

He squeezed her arm, and said he would send her his offer in writing.

After the men left it was getting late, Gordon suggested he would take her out for dinner. Nancy was rather surprised, as it was a long time since he had suggested this.

He took her to the George Hotel in Haddington for dinner; she was glad it was not North Berwick and the Marine Hotel. He seemed to be in a good mood, and talked about the meeting that afternoon. It had been a long day, and he suggested she should stay the night and not drive home. She agreed, and they made their way back. She was tired, but she accepted a dram as a night cap before retiring.

Gordon suggested that she should sleep with him, as he was missing her, and she gave in. He had drunk two or three glasses of whisky, so she knew he would probably fall asleep before she came to the bedroom. It had been a while since she had had sex with him; it was not like going to bed with Bob.

Gordon was not asleep; he was waiting for her to slip in beside him. He took her in his arms and kissed her softly on the lips. The whisky had certainly relaxed her, and she kissed him back.

Afterwards Nancy stared at the ceiling, wondering if she should she accept Mr Turnbull's offer, but if she left her employment with Gordon, how on earth would he cope, and find another secretary?

The next day it was business as usual, but Nancy decided to have a swim before going home. She made her way to the pool, where she changed into her costume before slipping into the water. She swam some lengths. Gordon appeared and stood watching her. She looked good in her costume with her long, slender legs, and he began to feel aroused. He knelt down beside her and kissed her.

"You look amazing in your costume, you are making me want to make love to you," he said, laughing a little.

Nancy smiled and climbed out of the water, placing a towel around her. "You should come in and have a swim; you'll feel the benefit from the exercise," she said. But he pulled her close to him and placed his hand on her breast.

"Let's make love here, it's nice and warm," he said, hugging her to him.

Nancy wondered what had got into Gordon; he had not been so randy for a long time. There was a lounger at the top end of the pool, and he took her hand and made for it. He slipped her costume off, placed her towel on the lounger, and pushed her down. He came quickly, not giving her a chance to have a climax. He stood up, zipping up his trousers.

She lay looking up at him. "I must get dressed now," she said, embarrassed.

"Of course, my dear, I'll make some tea, come to the conservatory."

Nancy was beginning to panic in case he insisted on her staying another night. She wanted to go home, as Bob might be phoning to make arrangements for the weekend.

She appeared at the door of the conservatory, wondering if she could make an excuse to leave. Gordon had poured the tea out, and handed her a plate of biscuits. She sat down, taking a biscuit and her cup of tea. She wondered if she should tell Gordon that she was seeing someone, as she did not want to have two relationships on the go.

"You know Nancy; I've really fallen in love with you," he said. "But I would like to know how your feelings are towards me."

Nancy stared at him; she did not want to hurt his feelings, but she did not love him. She cleared her throat and said,

"Gordon I am your secretary, not your wife. You are making it difficult for me to work for you, when you say such things. I am fond of you, but am not in love with you. You must understand how I feel."

"Of course, I am sorry for taking advantage of you at the pool. I really thought you enjoyed having sex with me, and I understand how you feel. I'll not say another word."

Nancy finished her tea as quickly as she could and told Gordon she had to go home.

She thought it would probably be best for her to accept Mr Turnbull's offer. It would get her away from Lisa and the family, and she would not have too far to travel, as the travelling was hard going from Edinburgh. She should just travel by train, and someone would pick her up as when she came for her interview. She would ask Bob's advice, but perhaps she should wait for Mr Turnbull's letter before she did anything.

She phoned Bob.

"Hello Bob. At a meeting yesterday afternoon, Mr Turnbull from Taylor Woodrow offered me a job working for them. I'm going to wait for his letter to see what salary he's offering, before I decide to give in my notice to Gordon. I know Gordon will be furious, but at least it will get me away from Lisa and family. What do you think?"

"I would wait and see before doing anything rash," he replied. "How are you feeling after the car chase? Anyway, I'll see you at the weekend and we will go somewhere exciting for a change."

"Yes I am so looking forward to seeing you again. I hope you're planning something very special, I can't wait for the weekend." She kicked off her shoes and put on her slippers. She wished her parents were still alive, as she would have asked her father for his advice. She said goodbye to Bob and hoped that the letter from Mr Turnbull would come soon.

Chapter 13

Lisa poured the liquid into a bottle and replaced the lid. She smiled to herself; this would do the trick. She lit a cigarette and gazed out of the window at the children playing with the dog.

Chasing Nancy down the lanes with Joe had been good fun, and Joe was so confident in driving, getting near her car yet not bumping into it. Nancy had looked terrified as she was being chased, but it was a good laugh. She hated Nancy, so proud and confident. It was no wonder her father was mesmerised by her. She wanted her mother to get back with her father, so it would be just like the good old days. She knew she should have studied at college, but she was lazy; she enjoyed parties, dances and flirting with the opposite sex. She didn't know how she had ever married David, but he had been so keen on her; he had chased her for nearly a year before she gave in to him.

David's family had not been sure at first if she was good enough for their son. David was so easy going and just liked watching sport on television, or going down to the local pub to meet his pals. At least she had two children; she knew her mother and father were proud of her for that.

Putting rat poison in Nancy's coffee and wine had not worked, but she knew Nancy had been ill after the wine, at David's birthday party. No one had noticed, which made it easier to double the dose. Nancy would become so ill that she could not work for her father ever again. If nothing else worked, she would invite her for a swim at her father' house, and then think of a plan to get rid of her once and for all. She knew her father couldn't swim, so he wouldn't be able to save her, and neither could David.

Lisa hid the bottle of rat poison in a safe place in the bedroom.

Doris clung on to Joe's arm as they walked through the meadows. It was a lovely sunny day as they made way north towards Princes Street. She had been in touch with Lisa about baby sitting at the weekend, so that Lisa and David could have a night out. This did not happen very often as Doris liked the good times, and really could not be bothered with kids.

Joe told her that Lisa had arranged to frighten Gordon's secretary, and the two of them had chased Nancy's car down the roads near Haddington. Doris looked at him.

"Chased her down the roads in East Lothian? You'd better be careful you're not caught by the police."

Joe squeezed her arm. "You know Lisa doesn't like her, she wants you and Gordon to get back together again. Anyway, we were only frightening her so there was no harm done." He chuckled, and Doris laughed as well. "You know of all the secretaries that Gordon employed, this is the first one he's fallen in love with. Maybe it's because she's not Scottish – she comes from South Africa."

"Never mind love I've got you, and you're no secretary" said Joe, laughing.

Doris hit him on the shoulder, but she also laughed. Doris was wondering if she could she get back with Gordon, although he was rather boring, liked to stay in at nights and watch television. He had a profitable business, and she could afford to have nice clothes and a sports car to run around in. She could still have a relationship with Joe, as he proved a great lover and was good company. She glanced up at him, smiling. She would have to be charming to Gordon, which could be rather difficult at times. Perhaps she could phone him and arrange a dinner date.

Gordon asked Nancy to go upstairs to fetch some folders he had left in a bedroom, as he needed to look at them urgently. Nancy had never investigated the rooms upstairs, but she was curious to find out what was up there. Besides the large lounge with good views facing north, there were four other rooms which were bedrooms.

She opened doors and had a good look around. She entered one room and walked towards a door which looked like a panel fixed to the wall. She pressed her hand on the panel and it moved inwards, showing a tiny room with a camp bed, a table and chair with a small window with no view except the roof. This must have been the maid's room years ago.

She heard Gordon calling and quickly slipped out of the room, placing her hand on the panel, so that it looked like a door again. She hurried downstairs with the folders he had asked for, and knew she could not ask him about the secret room. She wondered if Gordon's family when they were children had been placed in that room when they were naughty. Of course, they had not lived here when they were youngsters, but she wondered why he should have a secret room. Did Lisa know about it?

She came down the stairs slowly in case she dropped the folders. Gordon was at the bottom, looking up at her. She said, "I've never been upstairs except the lounge, sorry to take so long." She felt guilty.

"That's all right. Perhaps I should have gone for the folders myself" he said, taking the folders from her. Nancy thought perhaps Joe was right; the house could indeed be haunted.

Chapter 14

Nancy was glad that the weekend had arrived, and suggested to Bob that they go for a walk. A walk by the sea would be healthy and good for them. He wondered why she suggested this, and suggested the Pentlands or Arthur's Seat in the centre of Edinburgh. He wanted to be beside her, although she was quiet about her work, and never mentioned Gordon or his daughter.

They drove out in his car and parked in the car park near Cramond. Nancy had brought a picnic, and they made their way over a bridge on to a grassy path. The weather was fine with a light breeze from the sea. She was glad she had worn a jacket and trousers. She held onto Bob's hand as they enjoyed the scenery. They managed to find a spot sheltered from the wind, and settled down on the rug to have their picnic.

Bob lay close to her, watching her take the goodies out

of the basket. She smiled at him, and handed over the bottle of wine for him to open.

"My god you think of everything, even the bottle of wine," he said. "No wonder Gordon finds you well organised."

She looked up at him and smiled. "That's my trouble – all my life I've been organised. Living in South Africa, we never knew if we were going to be burgled or attacked."

"Nancy you have had quite a life. You must find me rather dull" he said, uncorking the bottle of wine.

People passed by, but they were in a sheltered spot, and no one could see them. They still had good views over the sea, but it was too cold to swim. Years ago Nancy had swum in the North Sea, but it very cold, and she did not stay in the water too long.

Nancy cuddled up to Bob and kissed him. He put his arms around her, and returned her kiss.

"How about having a meal in a hotel before we make for home?" she said, tucking in to a sandwich.

"Good idea, saves cooking, my place tonight to stay. If we stay at your place, Gordon might turn up like he did when your friend was staying. I bet that was a shock to the system."

Nancy laughed. "Well, you could say that. Let's not talk about him or his ghastly family."

After their picnic they walked further along the coast before returning to the car. Nancy was feeling tired with all the fresh air, and she lay back in the car and closed her eyes as Bob drove.

Suddenly a car shot out in front of them and Bob had to brake. The car swerved from side to side, and Bob wondered if the driver was drunk. Bob followed the car, keeping his distance. Nancy was fully awake now; she glanced back to see if any cars were following them.

"My god, that's Doris's car." Nancy said. "Can you make out who is driving?" She put her hands over her face, wondering if she was dreaming.

"Honey, this is no dream. Someone is out to have a good time, probably someone juvenile."

They continued as if they were going to Newhaven, but Bob managed to cut down a side road. Nancy looked to see where the car went, but it had disappeared.

"This really is serious, I'm going to report this to the police. Did you manage to get the registration number?" he asked Nancy.

"No. It was going too fast, but it was a dark blue sports car. What shall we do now?"

"The first thing is I am reporting this episode to the police, and you, my girl, will change your job. We can't go on like this – you're becoming a nervous wreck. Why on earth did you suggest coming out"

Nancy did not reply. She knew it was Doris's car, but who was driving it at such dangerous speed?

"I told you I had an offer from Mr Turnbull from Taylor Wimpey?" she said. "At the last meeting, he offered me a job. I was rather taken aback, but I think he noticed that working for Gordon was becoming a strain, as he was losing his temper quite a lot."

"I tell you what we are going to do; we are going to go home. I can't report this incident without the registration number of the car. Are you sure it was hers? Come on, you can stand up for yourself. Gordon won't bite, it's the daughter you have to watch and perhaps that Joe who works for him. I know you don't like him,"

Nancy kept quiet and did not say anything.

Nancy was glad when they got to Bob's apartment, and accepted the drink he gave her. They sat side by side, not speaking but enjoying the peace and quiet of the late afternoon.

"Please, think hard about accepting Turnbull's offer of employment," said Bob. You are in a rut with Gordon, not that he is a bad sort of person, but I don't think he realises what really is going on with his daughter's deception. Promise me you will give in your notice."

Nancy knew that Bob was right, and that she had to put on a brave face and give her notice to Gordon. She would do it first thing on Monday morning.

"Now, come here you gorgeous creature and give me a hug and a kiss" said Bob, pulling her towards him. Nancy floated into his arms, placing her arms around his neck and giving him a long kiss. She did not want to go anywhere that evening, not to the cinema or theatre, just to relax and be with Bob.

He cooked a meal of steak and chips, with ice cream to follow. He was a good cook, and she realised that men liked cooking; even her husband had done a lot of the cooking when she was married. She was definitely worried about going back to work on the Monday, and could not help thinking how Gordon would react to her notice.

Looking back over the months she had worked for Gordon Mackenzie, she wondered why his daughter hated her so much. She usually got on well with fellow workers, except perhaps for females who either were jealous or very friendly. She thought of that weird room off one of the bedrooms at Gordon's. Why was there a camp bed, table and chair placed in it?

She woke up suddenly wondering where she was, feeling her face covered with sweat. She was having a nightmare, and felt Bob's arms around her comforting her.

"Hey, you're having a bad dream" he said, cuddling her.

"Oh I am so sorry I woke you, I was having a nightmare, it was so vivid, I was trying to get away from Joe, Doris and Lisa who were chasing me up the stairs to that awful room. I was running for my life." She wiped her face with her hand. "I do hope dreams don't come true, do they?"

"No, of course they don't" he said, holding her tight. He kissed the top of her head, pulling her close to him. They fell asleep in each other's arms.

Nancy did not want the weekend to end, and the thought of going to work on the Monday really depressed her. She only hoped that Gordon would accept her resignation without making a great fuss. The salary she was receiving from Gordon was far superior, but Mr Turnbull's offer was a decent one. and it would get her away from the Mackenzies, including Joe and Lisa.

The next morning after a large breakfast, Nancy and Bob took a walk up Arthur's seat. Nancy only liked walking on straight roads, not up steep hills or mountains. Her late husband had liked hill walking and mountaineering and had joined a walking club.

Nancy returned to her own place early Sunday evening. She sat watching the television, but not really paying attention to the show. She got up and sat at her desk, and taking up her pen she started writing her notice. Should she really be doing this? She had been working for Gordon for nearly four months, and was she all that happy to be working for him. She did not want to have to keep looking over her shoulder to see who was following her, with Lisa trying her best to kill her. Bob was right she was becoming a nervous wreck working for Gordon, and trying to avoid his amorous advances. She had never in her life come across this situation before. Had the other secretaries left because of Gordon's amorous advances? She shook her head and told herself that she was doing the right thing in giving in her notice.

She wondered how her relationship with Bob would last, because he was still married, and she was older than he was. She knew at this time of her life that she could not have any children. But he was so understanding, and she really did love him, loved his jokes, his outlook on life, and he was so different from Christopher. She shook her head, closing the drawers of her desk, and got up. She would think about this tomorrow.

Chapter 15

Nancy parked the car at Gordon's and made her way into the house. She was nervous at meeting him, as she knew Bob was right that she was becoming paranoid about Lisa and being poisoned. Of course, she had to have proof that Lisa was actually putting poisons in the drinks. She also knew that Gordon would stick up for his daughter, and tell her it was all in her imagination.

She sat looking at the computer and the files beside her. She stared out of the window and jumped when Gordon spoke to her from the doorway.

"Good morning my dear. How are you today?" he said, coming up to the desk.

"Sorry I never heard you come in, I am well" she said, staring at him. She had to tell him that she was not happy working for him anymore, and had been offered a post of secretary with a building company. He handed some files to her, and asked if she could possibly type them up as soon as possible.

"I need to speak to you Gordon, when will it be convenient?" she asked. But then the phone started ringing. He walked out of the room, holding up his hand as if he wanted her to be quiet. She opened the files and started typing. He poked his head in and said "I'll see you for coffee," then disappeared.

She was taking a chance, as she had been in touch with Mr Turnbull about his offer for the post of secretary. She had not actually accepted his offer yet, but she could bluff her way, informing Gordon that she had.

Time passed, and at 10.30 am Gordon came in and told her to come through to the conservatory for coffee. She nodded and felt she was probably being rather mean to suddenly make this statement regarding handing in her notice.

Gordon was lighting up a cigar and gazing out of the window when she came in to the room. "Hello Nancy, did you want to see me about work?" he asked, looking directly at her. She lifted her cup, hoping he would not notice her hand shaking.

"Gordon I've been offered a post as secretary to Mr Turnbull at Taylor Wimpey" she said.

There was a pause. Gordon put his coffee cup down and looked at her. It seemed he had not taken in what she had said.

"Have you accepted? And when did this come about?" asked Gordon, looking at her. Nancy sipped her coffee, praying that he would not make too much fuss.

"I've not exactly accepted his offer yet, as I'll have to give you notice. Is it a month's notice that is required?" she said.

There was silence. Gordon stood up and came over to sit beside her. Nancy finished her coffee and looked at him. She could not tell if he was angry or amused at her little speech.

He placed his hand on her arm and said, "It does seem that I've not been paying enough attention to you, when colleagues start offering you work. Are you not happy, or is my salary not high enough for you? I wonder what Mr Turnbull offered that I cannot give you. If I knew what his offer was, I would double it. I don't want you to leave Nancy, you are a marvellous worker."

Oh no, she thought. How on earth was she ever going to leave?

She sat up straight and looked at him and said.

"Gordon, it is not the salary, but I feel I need to move on. Besides, your family are not all that friendly towards me, especially your daughter."

He laughed and said, "You must not take any notice of Lisa; she is like her mother and ambitious in all the wrong ways. I know she wants me to get back with her mother, but there has been too much water under the bridge. I want you to stay and work for me. No butts. I think our relationship has grown into something wonderful for me, but perhaps you don't feel the same way."

"Gordon, please tell me if it's a month's notice that I have to give you. I know Lisa hates me and is jealous. I was happy to begin with, but over these months; I've become frightened for my life."

"Frightened for your life? What do you mean, my dear?" He looked shocked. Nancy knew she had to tell him; otherwise she would be a prisoner for the rest of her life.

"Gordon, listen to what I am saying. It has not been my imagination, but I've been poisoned twice, and chased around East Lothian in my car, by a blue Land Rover. I'm becoming a nervous wreck."

He looked rather confused. "I'll ask my family what's going on, and I'll get to the bottom of this. I am going to phone Mr Turnbull, and ask why he wants to employ you."

He pulled Nancy towards him and kissed her on the forehead. "Now my dear, go and type out those documents."

Nancy felt like a naughty school girl being dismissed by the headmaster. She went to the room and phoned Bob. She knew it was useless talking to Gordon any further, as he was not going to listen to her.

She was told that Bob Jones was out of the office, but would phone her when he returned.

She was nearly crying over the papers on her desk, angry that Gordon did not want her to leave. She was trapped in an environment that was not so easy to get out of. And of course, Lisa would deny that she was poisoning her.

The hours went by slowly and Nancy kept looking at the clock, hoping that time would fly by. She certainly did not want to stay another night with Gordon; she had to refuse all his invitations, even dinners at the various hotels nearby.

Gordon spent most of the day out somewhere, and she hoped she could leave before he returned. Perhaps he had gone to visit one of his sisters for her advice about Nancy.

Sam came over with some files and asked if she could file them in her office cabinet. She was pleased to see him, and asked him how the projects were coming along. He told her they were coming to an end, and he had to work out the expenditure for the land that Gordon had recently bought. Sam was not one for gossiping, and he wished her a good afternoon and returned to the offices across the way. She was relieved that Joe had not come over to stare at her, making remarks and being very rude.

Nancy finished all the typing of the documents, and for the rest of the time she looked at one of the magazines she had bought the other day. Then the phone went and she lifted the receiver.

"Good afternoon Gordon Mackenzie's," she said.

"Mrs Lockhart, this is Mr Turnbull speaking. Have you considered the post I offered you?"

Why was Mr Turnbull phoning her on the office phone? She licked her lips and crossed her fingers before answering. "Yes Mr Turnbull, I may have to give a month's notice to Gordon. I've mentioned that I wished to leave his employment, but I'm not sure how he has taken this news. Has he been in touch with you?"

"No, not yet, I wanted to make sure that you were happy to leave his employment and come and work for my company. If you have to work a month's notice, so be it. Please don't worry yourself my dear; I know Gordon can be difficult. I'll send the necessary documents for you to look at and do think hard about leaving Mr Mackenzie's employment."

Nancy placed the phone back on its cradle and glanced at the clock. Gordon had not returned, so she grabbed her coat and made her way to her car. She noticed Joe looking out of the window at her, and saw him lift his hand to wave at her. She closed the car door and moved off, before he could come out and started talking to her.

She arrived home safely just as the phone was ringing. She hoped it was Bob and not Gordon, who probably wanted her to stay over.

"Hello" she said, "Hello gorgeous. How are you today, and how did it go with Mackenzie?" asked Bob.

"Hello Bob, thank god it's you and not Gordon. I did hand in my notice, butI may have to work a month's notice. I'm not sure how he has taken it, and anyway, I hardly saw him today. Mr Turnbull phoned me to find out if I was accepting his offer, and I told him I might have to work a month's notice. I think Gordon will double the salary so he can keep me working for him."

"That's my girl. Please don't worry, everything will work out, you'll see. Anyway, how about going out for dinner this Friday?"

Nancy needed cheering up. "That would be wonderful, something to take my mind off work and the Mackenzie family. See you on Friday."

Bob blew a kiss down the phone She sat down on the sofa, put her feet on the footstool and hoped that Friday would come soon.

Chapter 16

Lisa just laughed when Gordon asked her about car chases and poisons. She knew he did not realise what she had been doing, so she pretended that she knew nothing about it. She certainly was not going to admit to him what she was really up to. He seemed to be obsessed with that woman Nancy, and probably thought he was in love with her. She knew Nancy was not too happy with work, and wanted to leave, which would get rid of her once and for all. She had got all this information from Joe.

Gordon had been in touch with Mr Turnbull regarding the offer he had made to Nancy. Mr Turnbull's reply was he thought that Nancy was a very good secretary, and perhaps needed a change after some months working for Gordon. Nancy held a meeting together and was extremely efficient in her work. He also told Gordon that he should not lose his temper so often, as it was embarrassing the other members at meetings. He said he was a very lucky man to have a secretary who never made a fuss.

Gordon was so angry he banged the phone down. How dare Turnbull tell him what he should do?

Nancy still did not get the answer she wanted regarding leaving Gordon's employment. Gordon never mentioned the subject, but she knew he was angry at the phone call to Mr Turnbull. She decided that she would give Gordon a month to find a new secretary. She phoned Bob to tell him that Gordon was not too happy with her planning to leave his employment. "If you are unhappy working in that environment, yes, do it, or you may never leave," Bob advised her.

Nancy thought he was right. He asked about Lisa and the family, but Nancy told him she had not seen any of them for some time.

Lisa thought she would pay a visit to her father and perhaps have a swim in the pool. She wondered if Gordon was having a sexual relationship with Nancy, and that was the reason he did not want her to leave. She thought it was quite disgusting that her father should indulge in such things. Dave, of course, never noticed what was going on in the family, so long as he could watch sport or go drinking with the boys.

Gordon was surprised to see his daughter up at the house. "This is a surprise. You don't usually come to see me during working hours. Is there anything wrong?" he asked, giving her a peck on the cheek.

She smiled and shrugged. "I thought I would come and see you, perhaps have a swim in the pool. You told me Nancy was a good swimmer. Is she here by the way?"

"No, she is not; she went home early after typing up all the reports. I can't fault her work. But she seems unhappy working here and Taylor Wimpey have offered her the post of secretary. I don't know what to do. I don't want her to go, she's a wonderful worker."

Lisa smiled and placed an arm through his. "Well Dad, perhaps you should let her go, if she is so unhappy. Maybe she is dating someone and wants to be with them. After all, you can't expect her to be always at your beck and call."

"What do you mean Lisa, is there something you're not telling me? I am very fond of Nancy, and I did think that she would accept my advances and marry me one day."

Lisa threw back her head and laughed. Gordon was smitten with Nancy, and it was not going to be easy to get rid of her. "Why don't you and Mum make it up and get together again?" she said. "Remember the good times you both had. Think about it Dad."

Gordon looked at his daughter and shook his head. "Water under the bridge my dear, we would only row and life would be unbearable. I know in your heart you would like

Doris and me to be together, but I'm sorry, it is not going to happen. Are you happy with David? Is your marriage working? You have wonderful children, look after them."

Lisa did not say anything after hearing that. She marched away to the swimming pool, where she swam a couple of lengths, and then sat with her feet in the water; she had to think of another way of getting rid of Nancy.

Nancy had invited Bob for a meal, as she wanted to tell him how Gordon had reacted to the news that she was leaving. She waited until they had nearly finished their sweet before she spoke of her morning with Gordon, and the vague answer he had given her.

"He seems horrified that I wanted to leave, and in fact he was insisting in doubling my salary," she said, pouring out the coffee.

Bob placed his hand on her arm. "Did you write out your notice or did you verbally tell him? Also, write to Mr Turnbull and accept his offer. You may on the other hand get another post with a different firm, where you will be happier."

They both burst out laughing.

"You're full of great ideas, but I don't really want to leave Edinburgh, it's been my home for so many years," said Nancy. "I've already worked down in London, that's where I met my husband. I'll write a letter later, as I'll have more time to think without too many distractions. Now it's getting late and I'll have to go. Let me know what you have decided, and I wish you all the luck in the world. Gordon does not own you, you're a free agent. You are not in love with him are you?" He started putting on his coat.

"No I am not, but he told me he's in love with me. It makes it an awkward situation, with his family hating my guts. I'll take your advice and do what you suggest. Anyway, I love you and not Gordon. At first, I was rather glad that someone had paid me such wonderful attention, after losing my husband, I never really had a social life after Christopher passed on." She put her arms around him.

"Well good night my sweet and I'll phone you tomorrow to see how you get on" said Bob, kissing her.

After swimming in the pool, Lisa made her way over to the offices to speak to Joe. Both men looked up when she appeared in the doorway.

"Hi guys, how is it going with the work?" She said, sitting on the edge of Joe's desk. She looked over at Sam. "I want to speak to Joe, Sam, do you mind leaving the room? Go and make a cup of tea or coffee, yes coffee, I fancy a coffee."

Sam shrugged and went through the back to fill the kettle. He wondered why Lisa had appeared; she rarely paid them a visit.

"What do I owe the company of a charming young lady?"

said Joe, grinning at her and lighting up a cigarette.

"Look, I've had this wonderful idea" she said, "Perhaps you may have heard that Nancy could be leaving Dad's employment soon. For a bit of fun why don't we kidnap her and keep her prisoner for a few hours in that secret room upstairs just to frighten her? What do you say?" She giggled, raising her eyebrows at him.

Joe looked at her and smiled, taking a drag from his cigarette. Where did she get all these ideas from? "We would have to be very careful that your dad's away from the house, and Sam, as we don't want folk spoiling our little plan do we?"

She laughed with him and then pressed a hand over her lips as Sam came in with steaming hot coffees. "What's all this hilarity, are you laughing at some joke?" said Sam, sitting down at his desk and looking at the two of them.

Lisa took her mug of coffee and shrugged, sitting down on a chair facing the two men. "You could say that. Anyway, I'd better go and say goodbye to father before I leave. Joe will see you soon, and don't forget our little talk. Maybe you have some suggestions. Bye Sam, and don't work too hard will you." She turned and went out of the door, blowing a kiss at the two men.

"What was that all about?" said Sam. "She never usually comes to see us, and what's all the secrecy?"

"Oh, you know she's full of high spirits. Perhaps she had taken something to make her laugh and giggle," replied Joe.

Joe and Doris often took drugs to make them feel happier, and Joe knew that Lisa also indulged, but David was a careful chap, loved his children and had a quiet life. Half the time David did not know what Lisa was up to.

Chapter 17

Nancy parked the car in her usual place at Gordon's. She picked up her handbag and touched the letter of dismissal in her hand. She felt nervous and wondered what kind of reception she would receive. She knew the lads across the way knew what was happening, as Sam would have got that information from Joe. They knew she was not all that happy working for Gordon, and she could see them looking out of the window.

She made her way to her room, where she found stacks of files all ready for her to work on. She brushed her hair, glancing at the mirror she held in her hand, and applied some more lipstick to her lips, as half the time she licked it off.

It was coffee time, and Gordon called her through to the conservatory, where he had the coffees and biscuits all set out. He smiled at her and handed her the mug as she sat down.

"I was in touch with Mr Turnbull by phone yesterday, and I thought he was rather rude to me. Of course, naturally he made a generous offer to you, but I made my offer even better so that you cannot refuse."

Nancy felt even more nervous as she handed him the letter, waiting to see if he was going to say anything more about it. He took it and placed it on the table in front of him. She gazed down at it, and knew it was not going to be opened until she left the room.

"Do you wish all the documents on my desk to be finished by this afternoon?" she said, drinking her coffee.

Gordon sat back and looked at her. "Yes, if that can be done, as I need them for the next meeting in a day or two. Don't rush, just take your time. I am going to look at some land that another housing builder is interested in, so I'll be back later on this afternoon. I would like to see you before you rush home, if you don't mind."

She knew that was the signal to leave, and hurried away back to her room. She had given a month's notice, hoping that within that time he could find another secretary. It was going to be difficult getting away and she knew he was offering a bigger salary so that she could not refuse it.

Gordon drove along the road thinking of Nancy, and wondering why she wanted to leave his employment. Was it because he had loved her as a woman and not as a secretary? And where would he manage to get another secretary who was as good as her? Maybe it was because of his family perhaps being rather hostile towards her, especially Lisa, who disliked her for some reason.

He looked at the envelope she had given him. What if she refused to carry on working for him? The money he was offering her was more than he could afford. What could he do if he lost her?

He stopped the car on arrival, opened the letter and gazed at the contents. She had given four weeks' notice, one month from yesterday's date. If he let her go, would she still be friends, perhaps be prepared to date as a couple? Maybe she was seeing someone, and that was why she had rushed home, to be beside him. He felt wounded at the thought, and was jealous of this man who had her affections. He felt like crying at the very thought of losing her. He wanted her to love him as he felt she had when he had first met her, but over time she had changed. Perhaps she was becoming bored with him and the work. He closed the letter and put it in his pocket. Two men had got out of their cars and were standing waiting for him.

Nancy phoned Bob to tell him she had handed in her notice, but Gordon had not looked at the letter, and now she was worried about what was going to happen. Suppose Gordon would not let her leave the house and kept her prisoner – what on earth was she going to do?

Bob told her not to be so dramatic; he could not do that, as it would be kidnapping.

"He could surprise you and tell you to pack your bags and go this afternoon," he said. "Please just see what offer he makes to you. I'll phone you tonight to hear what he says."

Nancy finished typing the reports, and noticed that the time was 16.30 hours. Gordon had not appeared, and she wanted to leave at five. Was he purposely keeping her waiting, out of spite?

She wandered around the room, wringing her hands and glancing outside to see if his car had returned. She noticed Joe coming over to the house, and sped back to her desk, sitting behind her computer and pretending to look at the folders. He knocked on her door and came in handing her a large envelope. She took the envelope from him and remarked. "Hello, is this very important?"

"It came this morning in the post, so as it's probably quite urgent thought I'd give it to you. Gordon hasn't returned. He will probably want to see you before you rush off," he added, smirking.

Nancy smiled sweetly at him and said, "Well, thanks for coming over, you must be really busy over at the offices."

He looked at her before replying. Was she being bitchy? She was so attractive. He felt like leaning over and kissing her hard on the lips, just to see what she would do.

"We are kept busy, as Gordon likes to keep everything up to date. You should know that by now."

She sat looking at him, hoping he would leave, but he stood still, staring at her. She got off her seat and came towards him. He grabbed her arm and roughly pulled her towards him, then placed his lips on her mouth and kissed her hard. She hit his shoulder, pushing him off, feeling she could not breathe. He grinned at her and said "I always want to do that to you, and I can tell you really enjoyed it." He turned away and went out of the door, still chuckling to himself.

Nancy sat down in shock. How dare he do that to her? Her mouth was sore, as he badly needed a shave and the roughness had hurt her mouth. She should have slapped his face, but he was stronger than she was. She went to the kitchen and made herself a cup of tea, and while waiting for the kettle to boil, she drank some water and rinsed her mouth out.

Gordon returned just after five o'clock, and rushed into the house, hoping she had not left.

"Nancy, are you still here?" he called, pushing the office door open. He was relieved to see her at her desk looking at a magazine. She looked up at him. She felt like saying "You're late", but thought she had better not say anything.

"Would you like some tea or coffee before you leave this evening?" he asked, hoping she would say yes.

"No thanks, I had a cup not so long ago. If there is

nothing else, may I leave now, as I don't want to get caught up in the traffic?" she said. She rose from her seat, lifting up her coat and bag.

"No, of course not. I'll speak to you tomorrow when I've time to think matters through."

They stared at each other, and he stood back as she passed him. She noticed the men had gone home, and she breathed in the fresh air before getting in to the car. She was thankful that for once he was not standing watching her as she drove away down the avenue.

Nancy was glad to get home from Gordon's, and she poured herself a gin and tonic, then sank into the sofa placing her legs up onto the coffee table. She placed her head back on a cushion, closing her eyes. She drifted slowly asleep and dreamt of her childhood in Scotland and South Africa. She remembered the house in South Africa with its large veranda and glorious aromatic gardens, and the wide, dusty driveway up to the house. The workers' houses were placed at the rear of the house, and to the side fields of vines stretched for miles. Her parents were members of a tennis and golf club and often spent their days playing, or mingling with the other members of the club. Nancy had enjoyed going there and playing with the other children when she was eight, drinking orange squash or playing hide and seek within the grounds of the club. Her parents took holidays down at the coast staying at a villa in Cape Town. She loved swimming in the sea, or adventuring up Table Mountain, where the views of the bay were magnificent. She often went to Port Elizabeth, where a snake charmer would play a tune on his pipe to encourage the snake to appear out of the basket. She also went to Durban, and remembered a very large swimming pool, which was very deep, which made her feel slightly scared to go into the water.

Her mother Margaret loved to go shopping, especially up to Durban, leaving her father to entertain her for hours. Margaret enjoyed needlework, and made Nancy's clothes when she was a child living on the farm.

Nancy was an only child, and it was only when her parents went to functions at the club that she was able to mix with other children. She did have one or two friends to stay overnight or on holidays, when they would climb trees and have midnight feasts, without their parents knowing what they got up to. She enjoyed her days on the farm, and when it was time for harvesting the vines to make the grapes into wine, everyone was ready to join in the hard work.

When Nancy was older she was sent home to stay with her grandparents Anthony and Mary Cummings in Forres, Morayshire, Scotland, where she attended the Academy.

Living abroad had not made it easy to bring up a child for schooling, although Nancy had attended a small school for European children run by a Miss Devine in Africa. At the Academy, she was placed in a class lower than she should have been in. At least she was not a boarder at the school, and she was grateful to stay with the grandparents, who spoiled her. Of course, she only went to Africa during the holidays, as her parents wanted her to do well at school and get good marks. After leaving school she did a secretarial course, and worked in various offices, before making her way down to London to work.

Her parents were delighted when she got engaged to Christopher, as both her parents had retired and were living in Edinburgh. They had sold the vineyard in Africa, and knew that it was time to move on and return to Scotland. The grandparents had passed away, and they sold the bungalow in Forres. They bought a house in an area called Churchill, a good residential part of Edinburgh where they settled down in their retirement. It was some time before Christopher and Nancy returned home to Edinburgh, where they bought a flat in Bruntsfield, and Nancy stayed there after her husband passed away.

Nancy woke up wondering where she was. She felt better after her nap, so she stretched her arms out, then got up and made herself a cup of tea. She had accepted Mr Turnbull's invitation to be a secretary to one of the directors' of their company, but she would probably have to work a month before leaving Gordon's. She wondered if she could stand working the full month, and if perhaps Gordon would not allow her to go. She knew that the guys working across from the house probably guessed that she would be leaving soon.

Did Lisa know as well? She would be the talk of the office for weeks to come with that Joe leering at her each time he saw her.

Gordon had not really spoken to her regarding her notice, and she wondered what she would do if he did not let her go. He could not hold her prisoner, yet she had this awful feeling that something was going to happen to her.

Chapter 18

Bob Jones took a sip of whisky as he sat watching television. He gazed out of the window, noticing that there was not much traffic going past. He opened a packet of Pringles and put one into his mouth, savouring the taste.

He thought of Nancy and wondered what it was she was afraid of about working for Gordon Mackenzie. Gordon was a serious sort of bloke with no sense of humour. Bob remembered the meeting when he had first laid eyes on Nancy. She had a lovely smile and appeared happy enough, but there was no opportunity to ask her out or really speak to her, and he did not ask for her telephone number, as she was swept away as soon as the meeting was over.

How long had she worked for Gordon? It must be at least four months; no wonder she was bored, and needed a change of scenery. The daughter sounded really selfish and clearly disliked Nancy. He remembered Nancy remarking that she thought Lisa was trying to poison her, but did Gordon know what was happening? Perhaps not, but Nancy had been quite close to Gordon when she first worked for him. Were they lovers, and did Gordon want to marry her?

He was so glad he had chatted her up at the business dinner, and he knew that she liked him; otherwise she would not have given him her telephone number.

He remembered his childhood with his brother Michael and sister Charlene. Michael was the eldest and was sent to Fettes College in Edinburgh. Charlene went to Mary Erskine's school, while Bob went to Melville College School, also in Edinburgh. His father was an architect in Aberdeen, before coming to Edinburgh to work. His mother was a nurse, and worked part time in a local hospital. Michael had joined the Royal Navy, as he was interested in travelling the world. He had married later in life, to a girl from Norway, and had three children, two girls and a boy.

Charlene had become a lawyer, and married a chap she worked with who was also a lawyer. She had one child and emigrated to Canada soon after her daughter was born.

Bob had taken his father's profession as an architect, but he was the wild one in the family, He liked women, and was always having affairs that never worked out. His parents worried about him, hoping he would settle down and meet someone and marry. This he did when he met Rita.

Rita was a redhead who came from Glasgow and was also an architect. She had no brothers or sisters, and as her parents had divorced when she was twelve, she came to stay with an aunt in Edinburgh. She was full of confidence and liked the good times, going out to dine and dance, and flirting with most of the men she met. Bob was jealous of her flirting, but she did not seem to care if she was his girlfriend. She was good for him and he knew that she really liked him, so after nine months, Bob took courage and proposed marriage to her, which she accepted.

Rita had settled down after the marriage, but Bob could not resist chasing women, which had put a strain on the marriage. After a few years, Rita had had enough of his behaviour; she had decided to leave him and applied for a post down in London. They were not blessed with children. Bob stayed on in Edinburgh, working in an architect's office. He missed Rita at first, but he continued to chat up women and have affairs, until he met Nancy. She was different from all the other women he had met. Nancy seemed to calm him and he really was happy and strong in their relationship. He felt it was a great pity he had not met her years before, otherwise he was sure that they would have married.

He had never felt this way before, with the excitement of seeing and meeting her, taking her out to dinner and parties, and best of all, making hot love to her. She was warm and funny and laughed at his jokes, yet there was sadness, which was probably due to her working for Gordon. He had to help her and give her strength to encourage her to leave her work, if she was that unhappy.

He took the phone and dialled Nancy's number. The ringing tone seemed to play out for ages, until at last she answered. "Hello" she said, sounding rather sleepy.

"Oh hi Nancy, just thought I would give you a call to see how you are. How did you get on at work? Did you hand in your notice, and what did Gordon say to it?" he asked.

"Yes and no. He didn't say anything, but he mentioned vaguely that he would offer me an extra bonus, so that I wouldn't take up the offer from Mr Turnbull. He doesn't want me to leave, but I really don't want to carry on working for him, as most of his family seem hostile towards me. I gave a month's notice, to give him time to employ another secretary. How are you doing these days? It seems ages since I last saw you."

"I miss you and want to kiss and hold you in my arms. Have you looked at other posts in the paper or job centres? Have you been asleep, did I disturb you?" he said, sipping his whisky.

"I'm tired and rather worried about going in tomorrow, as I know Gordon has a temper and he'll try his best to persuade me to stay on" she said, pulling the dressing gown closer to her chest.

"Look honey, everything will turn out in the end, just be strong and don't let him bully you. I'll take you out this weekend and we'll have a good time. By the way, does he know about me?"

"I've not mentioned you by name but I did tell him I was

seeing somebody. I honestly think it will be hard for me to break away from the Mackenzie family, although Lisa will be over the moon if I leave." She tossed her hair back.

"Don't worry my love, I'll let you go now, try and rest and have a good night's sleep," said Bob.

"I'll try and not think of what is going to happen, but I have this awful feeling that soon something is going to happen to me" she said, standing up and pacing around the room. She was worried, because she knew Gordon could turn quite nasty towards her and prevent her from leaving.

"Nothing will happen to you my sweet, just try and relax and I'll be in touch with you tomorrow" he said. He had an uncomfortable feeling that she could be right, and he was determined to keep in contact with her. Surely Gordon would not be stupid enough to keep her against her will? But now he was beginning to imagine dreadful things. Perhaps he watched too many thrillers on the television.

She said goodnight to him and went to the bedroom to have an early night. She picked up the book she was reading, hoping that it would occupy her mind and calm her down.

That night she dreamed that she was running downstairs with Gordon, Lisa and Joe running after her. They were getting nearer and nearer to her, and she fell down the last few steps, glancing back to see how near they were to her. She ran for the door, but it was locked, and turned to face them, fearing the worst. They stopped before her and Joe advanced, grinning, with a knife in his hand. She looked sideways and ran towards the back door hoping that it was not locked. She could hear their footsteps running after her. Then she grabbed the handle of the door and threw it open, before rushing out and making for her car. She felt in her pocket to see if she had her car keys, and used the remote control to open the door. She slid into the seat without putting the safety belt on, then started the car. They were grabbing at her door and banging on the window, and she pressed her foot on the accelerator and turned the wheel, so the car swerved around in a semi circle and flew down the avenue and out onto the main road. She did not stop until she made it home.

Nancy woke up with sweat pouring off her, her night dress soaked, she got up and went to the bathroom to wash and change her clothes. She looked in the mirror, and thanked god that it was only a bad dream.

Chapter 19

Nancy got out of her car and slammed the door shut. She gazed around, hoping that Joe and Sam would notice her arrival. She was mad that Joe had kissed her, but she blamed herself for approaching him. She walked slowly towards the house, feeling nervous and wondering what Gordon would say to her. She knew he was going to offer her a larger salary, but she was determined that she would not accept any offer.

She opened the door of her office and sat down, looking out of the window to see if the two men were watching her. The whole house was silent, and she looked out at the passage but nobody was there, where was Gordon? She decided to check the conservatory and kitchen, but the rooms were empty. There were no files on her desk, and she looked out of the window to see if there were any other cars there. The whole place seemed to be deserted. She hated doing nothing, but she and knew that it was Thursday and there was a meeting at 14.00 hours with Persimmon Homes.

She sat for what felt like an hour before she heard the door opening and saw Gordon appear. He smiled at her and said "Good morning. Come and have a nice cup of coffee before we discuss the meeting." He headed off towards the kitchen, and she gathered up her belongings and followed him. She stood in the doorway, watching him place mugs and sugar onto to a tray. He turned and smiled.

"How are you today, you are very quiet, are you feeling all right?" He asked, glancing at her.

"Yes I'm fine" she said, and followed him into the conservatory. She made sure she sat opposite him and not beside him as she usually did. She took the mug of coffee and took a sip. She looked at him over her mug, waiting for him to speak.

"This meeting is going to be a rather difficult one for me; as I am not going to accept their proposals, even though they could be reasonable" he said, looking at her.

"I'm only the secretary not the boss, and if you would like to me to type up any refusals I'll do it, until you find someone suitable for the job."

She could not believe what she had just said and nearly choked over her coffee. He stared at her for a moment, clearing his throat before replying.

"Nancy, Nancy, come on dear you are my secretary. You are the best worker I've ever had, better than the two men over there, who I know play games on their computer. Why do you want to leave a good job with a salary you would not get anywhere else?"

She looked at her hands, and covered them so that he would not notice them shaking. She looked at him and thought, no, even though he offered marriage, she would not accept.

"I've spent at least four months here working for you, and I feel that I would like to move on and do other things," she said.

"So Nancy, are you not in love with me? I think you are a wonderful person and I loved you the first time I saw you. Can you believe that? You were so loving in the early days, and you admit you have a boyfriend now, even though you want to leave and do the things you want to do. I feel I must let you go, if that is what you want to do. I am older than you and must not really hold you back, even though my family will be sorry that you want to leave."

Nancy could not believe her ears; he was going to let her go. She smiled at him and placed a hand on his arm.

"I'm sure that some of your family will be pleased," she said. "Your sisters were friendly, but not your daughter. Somehow she disliked me the moment she saw me and was very rude. I don't know why, only that she didn't want me to marry you, and perhaps I might have done when I first met you. I had been widowed for a good number of years, and was so glad that I had met someone to love."

He placed his hand over hers, giving it a squeeze. "Now

we must get ready for this afternoon's meeting. I note that you have given a month's notice, and wondered if you had anyone in mind to be my secretary."

"No, I'm afraid I don't have anybody in mind, but you could apply to a secretarial bureau who will supply you with a temp to begin with." She was feeling so relieved.

She rang Bob as soon as she returned to her office, and left a message telling him that Gordon had accepted her resignation.

She was surprised how nice Gordon had been over letting her go. She wondered if he would tell his family right away or leave it to the weekend. She knew Lisa would be over the moon, and hoped that whoever took the post of secretary would be treated fairly and respectfully.

The meeting went smoothly and Gordon refused their offers, although they were pretty good, so Nancy typed out the refusals, hoping that whoever took her place would realise that Gordon worked in mysterious ways. As her work was up to date, she informed Gordon that she was going home and would see him tomorrow, hoping he would not ask her to stay and have supper with him.

From the window, Joe and Sam watched her getting into her car. She glanced towards them, giving them a vague wave as she passed. She felt free and the thought of leaving this place and never returning was going to be wonderful. Roll on three and a half weeks from now.

"I wonder why she's looking so happy," said Joe.

Sam was looking at some papers. He looked up. "I don't know why you're so concerned about Nancy, perhaps you fancied her, but were afraid to ask her out."

Joe drew on his cigarette and laughed. "She's a stuck up bitch, no mistake about that. Doris didn't like her and Lisa hates her."

Sam sat back and looked hard at Joe. "Maybe you don't have to worry, because it's my guess she has handed in her notice. You know, I actually overheard Gordon cursing her the other day, when one of his sisters was paying him a visit. He told her that Nancy wanted to leave his employment after all these months, and what was he to do now? I bet twenty quid that she does leave." He smiled at Joe.

"Well you're on, and I bet she doesn't leave. You know he's crazy about her, it'll be hard for him to let her go."

"Look out, here he comes now. Keep your mouth shut regarding Nancy" said Sam.

Gordon entered the building, looking at the two men.

"I've brought some work that urgently needs doing right away. That will keep you two busy and not gossiping about my staff," he said, placing the papers on the table in front of Sam. "There's too much playing about here, and not enough work being done. I want these papers completed by noon tomorrow, so heads down, no talking and get on with it."

They looked at each other and Sam opened the folder. Gordon walked out and made his way to his car.

"Where's he going?" said Joe.

"Come on, you heard what the man said, let's get working before he changes his mind and gives us the sack," said Sam.

"Well something has upset him. I bet it was Nancy" said Joe, puffing at his cigarette.

"Come on man, just keep your head down and work. Forget your women for a while at least" said Sam.

Gordon pressed his foot down on the accelerator and zoomed down the driveway and out on to the main road. He had no idea where he was going to, but it would be anywhere far from the house and the two men. He knew they were talking about Nancy, like two old women, and wanted to find out if it was true that she was leaving. How could she do this to him? Perhaps he had been too busy with work to really pay attention to her, and she had found someone else to love.

He drew into a side road and cut the engine. He put his head on his hands over the steering wheel, and felt the tears falling down onto his hands. Why could she not stay and work for him? God knows where he was going to find another secretary. How could Nancy do this to him? He should have married her, and then she would not have gone off and fallen in love with someone else. How was he going to tell his sisters, who thought Nancy was wonderful, and his daughter and the family?

No, he would wait a while; after all, she was not leaving for another month. He knew he was not an easy man to work for or even live with, and that was why his marriage to Doris had broken down. Doris had done nothing to educate herself into a better life, instead of lying around the house. He knew she wanted them to get back together again and be happy families. Lisa of course, wanted her mother to marry him again so it would be just like the good old days.

He looked at himself in the mirror and wiped the tears away with his handkerchief. *Come on, grow up*, he muttered. He started the engine, and made towards Haddington to visit Ursula. She would understand, and she could advise him how to get another secretary.

Chapter 20

Joe took a drag from his cigarette and looked at Doris, who was lying beside him. She turned her head and gazed at him.

"So Nancy's leaving," she said. "I wondered how long it would take her to get fed up and go. Not that I blame her for leaving him, he is the biggest bore."

She laughed and drew on the cigarette Joe passed to her.

Joe giggled. "Lisa has this great idea," he said. "Just for fun we should kidnap Nancy and put her in the small upstairs room."

Doris smiled. "That's a dangerous idea, I certainly wouldn't like to be kidnapped and put in there. How long are you keeping her in there? Gordon's always at home and he could become suspicious."

Joe turned to her and gave her a kiss, which she returned. She sighed and said, "You know Lisa has the most extraordinary ideas, she must look at that television all day while David's out working. You did tell me that she had tried to get rid of Nancy by putting something in her drinks, which is dangerous – she could be caught and sent to prison. Perhaps you should talk to her, because Nancy will have left before you and Lisa start this dangerous scheme." She took another puff of her cigarette and slipped out of bed, placing a dressing gown around her shoulders. Joe caught her hand, pulling her back to kiss her again.

"It'll be okay. Don't you worry your pretty head about Lisa or Nancy; everything will work out. It's not as if we're going to kill her, we won't go as far as that."

"Gordon always seemed to have trouble with his secretaries," said Doris. "He would try to get engaged to them, and they fled. He obviously thinks he has fallen in love with this one, and she wants to leave and move on. I don't blame her." She poured a cup of coffee and drank some.

"If you don't agree to our little scheme, you don't have to worry," said Joe. "I won't tell you the day or time we're going to do it. We'll make sure Gordon's out of the house."

He put out the cigarette and poured some coffee.

Doris shrugged. "Well, I don't think you should do this to her. After all she has been a good secretary to Gordon, probably the best he has ever had."

"Well, I never thought that you would stand up for this woman," said Joe. "I thought you hated her like Lisa does."

Doris looked at him and without a word went to the bathroom.

Lisa was lying on the couch watching a film when the phone rang. She got up and put the receiver to her ear. She said, "Hello, who is speaking, is that you Joe?" She knew it was not her husband, as he was not back from work.

"Lisa, it's Joe here. I was speaking to Doris, and she thinks it's madness to take Nancy prisoner. She thinks we should not go through with it."

"You know Mum's afraid of everything," Lisa replied. "Anyway, it has nothing to do with her, I'm surprised you mentioned it to her. She'll probably go and warn father. Nancy won't be leaving for another month, so we have plenty of time. I've got another surprise up my sleeve, and I'm not going to tell you anything about it."

She pulled a cigarette out of a packet, placed it in her mouth and lit up. Men! Why was Joe being so difficult? He was the only one she could trust to help her.

"Are you there?" said Joe, wondering if she had put the phone down on him. She blew smoke and replied, "Yes, I'm here. Are you in or out Joe? I could do this by myself. David and the children must not know anything about this or the family. Do you hear me?"

Joe took a deep breath and wondered why he bothered with women; the trouble was, he loved them. "Oh come on Lisa, don't be a wimp. You know I'll help you, look what we've done so far, this could be good fun." He heard her chuckle. He knew she relied on him. He finished the call.

Lisa poured herself a Martini, although she knew she should not be drinking, as David would be angry with her if he caught her, especially during the day. Joe would help her, she could depend on him, but her mother was being awkward. Why had Joe told her about their plans? Nancy was not leaving for a month, and this had to work out. She knew her father would be furious that his precious woman was hurt, but when Nancy left and he got another woman, would she be as glamorous as Nancy?

Sam lifted the papers he had brought home to study. They weren't complicated, and the plans looked good, but how much was it going to cost? Persimmon Homes had applied for permission to build more houses on the plots laid out on the land near North Berwick, and it was up to Gordon Mackenzie to accept them. Gordon was a canny man; he never accepted builders' ideas unless he was going to profit from them himself. He poured the rest of his beer into a glass, and took a sip. The beer was good.

He wiped his mouth with the back of his hand. He sat for a while and his thoughts went to Nancy. She was leaving, and he was sure Gordon was not amused about losing her. She was an excellent worker, never said much, and perhaps it was wise to keep her mouth shut. He did not know much about Gordon's family. He knew he had two married sisters and a daughter with two children, who came once in a while to visit or swim in the pool. He was glad he was not working in the house.

He looked at his watch and knew it was time to go into town to do some shopping before it was too late. He did not like weekends; he had a few friends, but they liked to go to the football, or sit in the house shouting at the television. His last girlfriend had only lasted for three months; she had thought him a bit dull, and moved on.

He wondered about Nancy. She had been married, but her husband had passed away some time ago and it was probably hard to find work at her age. She was an attractive woman, and it was no wonder Gordon found her a good secretary, and was attracted to her. She probably had a boyfriend, and was perhaps thinking of remarrying. He wondered why he was thinking of her. Maybe he fancied her, but she would not be bothered with a chap like him. He knew Joe always made rude suggestions about her, and probably fancied her too, but then he had a relationship with Gordon's ex wife. What a funny world we live in.

He folded the papers, reached for his coat, and went out of the door.

Chapter 21

Nancy sat drinking a cup of coffee and looking at a magazine she had bought the other day. She thought she had really done it now, giving in her notice to Gordon, whom she could tell was a bit upset at losing her. She had been in touch with Taylor Wimpey about accepting Mr Turnbull's invitation to work for them, and a contract had been sent to her for signing.

She thought about her relationship with Bob Jones and wondered where it was leading. He was still married to Rita, and had never bothered to get a divorce. Since Christopher's death she had never really bothered to go out socially except with a few girlfriends. While she was working for Gordon he was all over her, expecting her to go here and there with him. Of course, she had been flattered at all the attention. The family with the spoiled daughter, and his sisters, who probably told Gordon how to woo her, hoping he would settle down and get married. Bob was right: she was better away from Gordon and his family, and the amorous Joe, who was always leering at her. She did not want to get married, well not yet; although she loved Bob very much indeed she could not see a future with him. Of course, working for Taylor Wimpey she would be based in Edinburgh, and would not have to travel miles over to East Lothian every day.

She had looked at other advertisements for a secretary through the papers and on line, other companies who paid well, and even a firm of architects, like Bob's. She would not work in the same office as Bob, as seeing each other at work would not be a good idea.

She phoned Bob and asked him over to her place for a meal that evening, as she wanted to make sure she was doing the right thing in leaving her job with Gordon. She knew Bob would convince her.

On the Monday when she returned to work, she found several cars in the parking area. She made straight to her room and sat down, waiting for Gordon to appear. She heard female voices, and gathered that his sisters were paying a visit to their brother.

"Oh my dear, you should not be worrying, she is sure to find something more suitable, and with a new secretary, work will flow in," Ursula was saying as she stood on the threshold before saying good-bye.

"Easier said than done my dear, it's all right for you to

talk, you know it's so difficult to find someone suitable to do this work. I am going to offer Nancy more money, so she cannot refuse. How am I going to get another secretary as good as her? I just don't know what to do."

"Stop fussing dear, just get on with it. If the poor lass wants to leave, let her go Gordon, you can't hold on to someone forever." She walked down the few steps and headed towards her car. "Good bye dear, speak to you soon."

Ursula got into her car and drove off.

Nancy peeped out of the window to watch Ursula leaving; she had heard every word that was said. She took out her lipstick and put it to her lips just as Gordon appeared.

"Morning Nancy, could you please come to the conservatory, I want to speak to you," he said, moving away. She knew he was going to offer her a larger salary. She followed him and sat down facing him.

"My dear, I am so sorry to hear that you are not happy working here, and I am at a loss about what to do. I want you to stay on working for me, and I am offering you two thousand two hundred pounds more on top of your salary. Please don't say anything, just hear me out."

Nancy licked her lips before answering.

"Gordon, my mind is made up. I've been offered a job with a building company, and I'll be starting work with them after my month is up here."

He shrugged, narrowed his eyes and looked at her. "So you are not happy, after all we have been through together. I cannot believe you want to leave me. Have you been dating someone and want to get married?" he asked, twisting his hands.

"I've been dating someone Gordon, but I would not say I was going to get married. That has nothing to do with work, and it's my business. I've been happy here, and found the work interesting, meeting different people." He appeared to be taking her departure very badly, but she was adamant that she was not going to be persuaded to accept his offer. She felt the atmosphere was getting rather tense.

"Have you anything for me to do this morning, as we have another meeting this afternoon?" She wanted this meeting to end, as she felt very uncomfortable.

He looked at her, and got up. "Yes, I have some work that needs doing, I'll give it to you, I am spending the morning over at the other office as I need to speak to the chaps about finance. See you later Nancy."

She left the room, glad to return to her desk. She knew it was not going to be easy leaving Gordon, as he was taking her news so badly.

The meeting went well, but she found it difficult to concentrate on what they were all saying. She kept thinking about what she was going to eat that evening, and then realised that Gordon was speaking to her. She looked at him, feeling embarrassed, and asked him to repeat what he had said to her.

"Nancy could you please type up these documents as

soon as possible, as they have to be posted out tonight." he said.

"Yes of course," she replied. She gathered up the files and as she passed, he grabbed her arm, holding it in a firm grip, which hurt her. She let out a cry and glared at him. "You are hurting me, let go," she said, but he still held her arm. He stared at her, and she wondered if he was punishing her for leaving.

"I don't want you to leave me, please think about what you are doing. I need you Nancy. We were such good friends when you came to work for me."

"I have to get these typed up" she said, and walked out of the room. It looked as if the Mackenzie family had a nasty streak, including the ex-wife and daughter. She wondered if she was ever going to get rid of them.

Chapter 22

The next day Nancy received a letter from Taylor Woodrow asking her to come for an interview at four o'clock on Friday. She had hoped to see Mr Turnbull, but on the letter it mentioned a Mr Thomson, a senior partner of the firm. She made an appointment at the hairdressers, to get her hair and nails done at the same time. She felt very nervous, as it was some time since she had had an interview; the last one was with Gordon.

She was shown into a lounge off the reception, which had seating behind a coffee table. She picked up a magazine, turning the pages but not really reading it. Time passed and eventually Mr Thomson's secretary, a thin woman with grey hair, asked her to follow her. They walked along a corridor with modern paintings on the wall, and eventually stopped outside a wooden door. The secretary knocked on the door, and Nancy was ushered into the room. A tall, balding man got up and came forward with his hand ready to shake hers. He smiled and she sat down opposite him.

He studied her for a moment before saying. "Mrs Lockhart, I see from your CV records that you are working for Gordon Mackenzie, and have been there for some months." She looked at him and replied. "Yes that is so." He turned over the pages of her file and looked up at her.

"May I ask what is the reason you want to leave Mr Mackenzie's firm? I see that you have an excellent record, and Mr Turnbull has recommended you, as he had observed that you are an extremely good secretary." He smiled at her.

Nancy licked her lips. She knew she had to be careful in replying to his question of her leaving Gordon's employment.

"Well, I've been at meetings with various building companies and your company, when we had meetings in Edinburgh and Mr Mackenzie's house. Mr Turnbull was often at meetings at Greenlands, and he surprised me by offering a post here with your firm."

"Yes, Mr Turnbull has suggested you join this firm, but before I offer you a post, you have already given in your notice to your present employer?" He folded his hands together, looking at her.

She looked straight at him and replied. "Yes, I've given a month's notice, to be fair to Mr Mackenzie, as it has given him time to look for another secretary."

He nodded and closed her file.

There was a knock on the door. It opened, and Mr

Turnbull looked in. He saw Nancy sitting there and immediately came forward to shake her hand.

"Oh Mrs Lockhart, how nice to see you once again. I hope Tom here is giving you all the news about our company" he said, glancing at Thomson.

"Yes of course I am" said Mr Thomson, a little flustered. He lifted her file, placing it to one side. The men looked at each other, and Mr Turnbull said. "Well Mrs Lockhart, I look forward to welcoming you into our company. Perhaps I should inform you that you could be meeting Mr Mackenzie at our meetings. I know he is a difficult man to work for, not always accepting our offers. Don't you worry about what I've just said – I'll make sure you don't meet him." He shook Nancy's hand, smiling at her.

Mr Thomson cleared his throat and said, "I was about to ask Mrs Lockhart to do a typing test, just for our records."

"Oh come on Tom, is that really necessary?" said Mr Turnbull. "I've seen what she has done at meetings; she is a very well organised lady." Nancy looked from one to the other and said, "It is perfectly all right to do a typing test, I know you would like to keep your records straight." She smiled at both men.

"Thank you my dear," said Mr Thomson. "Vivien will show you the ropes." He shook her hand.

Nancy was shown into an office where computers stood on several tables. She sat down at one and was given a page to type out. Vivien, the secretary, sat at another desk and carried on typing. Nancy typed away and finished in good time. She looked at Vivien, who came over to look at what she had done.

"That's good, no doubt Mr Thomson will be in touch with you in a few days time," she said.

Nancy gathered up her coat and handbag and left the office. Just as she reached the pavement outside, she heard Mr Turnbull calling her. She turned to find him waiting for her.

"Oh Mrs Lockhart, just a quick word before you go," he said. "How is your friend Mr Jones? You remember at the cocktail party some time ago?"

She was taken aback by this. "Yes, we are still good friends," she said, wondering why he had brought up that subject. "He works in an office in George Street."

Was he trying to find out if she was engaged to Gordon? He seemed embarrassed and shook her hand as if he was dismissing her. She took his hand, smiling at him, and turned away, making her way home.

As soon as she was home she kicked off her shoes and put her slippers on, glad to sit down and put her feet up. The phone rang; she got up to answer it. "Hello," she said.

"Hello Nancy, Gordon here. Just wondered if you were doing anything this weekend?"

She sat down and said "Yes, I am going out with friends, why do you ask?" She closed her eyes for a moment and waited for his reply.

"Oh, I thought you would have liked to come over here, and we could have gone out for a meal" he said, sounding disappointed. Was he going to be a nuisance phoning her up, just because she was going to leave his employment?

"Sorry Gordon, thanks for your invitation, but I am busy all weekend," she said, knowing that on Saturday, she would be with Bob.

He sighed. "I'll see you on Monday then my dear. Enjoy your weekend."

On the Monday Nancy arrived at Gordon's and proceeded to her room, where she sat down behind her desk. She had three weeks to go before she left his employment. The nightmare she had had the other night felt so real, and she looked at the offices where the men worked to see if she could see them. The place looked deserted; there were no lights on and no sign of Gordon.

She made her way to the downstairs bedroom and opened the door of the wardrobe, where she had collected some belongings she had left there. She put a couple of items of clothing and a make-up box into a holdall. She heard Gordon calling her, and she rushed back to her room and placed the holdall under her desk. He appeared at the door and said. "Oh there you are, I was wondering where you had got to." He smiled at her.

"Yes, here I am ready to carry on the work. I noticed that there was nothing on my desk to type out." If there was nothing to do, perhaps she could go home.

"I would like you to come with me for a drive, as I want to show you some land I am thinking of buying," he said. She licked her lips and replied, "I'll get my coat and bag," then came around her desk to join him.

Gordon had taken the Land Rover and they drove west. Neither spoke. Nancy stared ahead, and wondered why he was so quiet. She wondered where they were going. Eventually they turned into a field which looked as though it had recently been ploughed.

"Here we are" said Gordon, and he opened the door and got out of the car. Nancy came up beside him. "I am sure you will agree that this land looks very healthy," he said, turning to look at her. She wondered why he was asking for her opinion, as she did not know anything about land. He continued, "What do you think of the potential of me buying this land for marketing for houses?"

She thought for a moment before replying. "You know Gordon, why are you asking me for an opinion? You know I'm a secretary not an architect or surveyor."

"My dear, if you are going to work for builders who build houses for people, you must have the knowledge of land and what type of houses they will build." She stood there and wondered why she was standing here listening to him talking about land and houses. She said, "I am sure Gordon you know best what you are doing, so do you think we could go now?"

He turned and looked at her. Then he placed his hand on her arm and squeezed it hard, making her squeal with pain. He pressed harder, and she had to bend her elbow to try and ease the pain. She yelled out, trying to get away from him. What was wrong with him? He had never done this before.

He gave her a weak smile, as if he had enjoyed hurting her. She made her way back towards the car, and felt in her pocket. Did she have enough money in case she had to get a bus back to the office?

He came up and stood by the car. "I thought it would be good to learn what you will be working on in the future, but now I know you are not all that interested in my work any more."

She wondered if she should walk away or get into the car, but this was right out in the country where there were no houses or shops.

"Get in the car," he said, opening the door. She quickly opened her door and sat down, looking straight ahead. He drove back like a madman, taking the corners on two wheels, and she had to hold onto her seat. When they arrived back, Nancy marched into the house without looking back at him. Gordon did not come into the house straight away, but went to see Joe and Sam at the office.

How was she ever going to have lunch with this man, who was so rude to her, and hurt her so much? She felt like crying, and made her way to the bathroom at the end of the hall, where she locked herself in and sat on the toilet and sobbed. She had to take a grip of herself, as she had a meeting in the afternoon, and knew she could not escape and return home.

Back in her room, she lifted her bag from under the table and looked through it, just for something to do with her hands. She did not see Gordon again until he called her to join him for lunch. What could she say to him? She did not want to make small talk, or ask him why he was so cruel to her.

She did not have to worry, as he spent the rest of the morning on the phone. She ate her sandwiches as quickly as she could. She wanted to go home, but there was the meeting with Persimmon Homes that afternoon and she had to stay to take some notes. She was furious with Gordon over his behaviour towards her; it was a great shock to her, as he had never done that before.

She found it difficult to smile at the men sitting opposite her at the meeting, but they did not notice any friction between her and Gordon. He was on his best behaviour, smiling around at everyone and talking about his new venture on the land he had seen that morning. The men seemed interested, and nodded their heads in agreement. Nancy poured out the tea and coffee and handed out the biscuits. She wondered if the men only came for the refreshments.

The meeting finished after an hour, and the men departed. Nancy rushed off to her room with the documents she had to type, as she did not want to be in Gordon's company. She typed furiously, her fingers hardly touching the keys. She had to keep calm and carry on as if nothing had happened, as she did not want to chat to Gordon over a cup of tea. As soon as she finished she would go home and relax with a stiff gin and tonic.

Gordon sat in the conservatory smoking his cigar, gazing at the cats sunning themselves on the wall. He knew Nancy was angry with him, but he was still annoyed that she was going to leave him and go somewhere else to work. He had offered her an extra bonus to stay on, but her mind was made up; she was in no doubt she wanted to leave.

He had taken Ursula's advice and contacted a secretarial agency for a temporary typist. The woman would turn up the following week. Of course, he had had three or four typists before Nancy had applied for the post, and they had been good typists, but were not all that interested in the work. How could she leave him in this position? And why was she so determined to leave? He smiled at the memory of their visit that morning to the land he hoped to buy; Nancy seemed to so negative. Was she not pleased for him and excited about his news. Of course, she wasn't, she was leaving his employment, obviously having never felt romantically attached to him.

He lifted up his phone to speak to his sister Jean. She would understand his feelings, and know how hurt he felt.

Sam came up the few steps to Nancy's office. She looked up at him as he as he appeared in the doorway.

"Hi Sam what can I do for you?" she asked, smiling at him. She liked Sam as he was always the gentleman.

He placed some papers on the edge of her desk and said. "I brought over these papers, and wondered if you could possibly type them up, the figures are all added up correctly. I need them before 5pm this evening."

Nancy took hold of the papers and glanced at the sheets. She hated typing figures, but as Gordon had not asked her to do this, she would do it.

"Yes I'll type these up for you Sam," she said. "Are you all doing OK?"

"We're doing fine. Getting several contracts finished, and waiting for Gordon to prepare the next one. I see you were busy with a meeting this afternoon." He cleared his throat, and looked out of the door towards the kitchen. "I hear you're leaving, and can I say I'll miss you? You're an excellent worker, and I want to wish you all the very best for the future. Also, can I say take care of yourself, especially before you leave here, as it's not as it seems." He shook her hand and left.

Nancy sat down and wondered about what he had said.

Was he trying to warn her about something? Was she in danger?

Gordon appeared and said "Come away now and have some tea, I've prepared some scones and cake. Did I hear voices, were you talking to someone?"

Nancy hoped he had not heard Sam's last sentence warning her. She followed him to the kitchen. He placed two plates of scones on the table, and some cake. She realised she was quite hungry, and tucked in.

He looked at her and smiled. "My dear, you must be starving, perhaps it was the country air that made you hungry," he said.

Nancy looked at him. "Sam came over with some documents, he wanted me to type them, and I said I would." He nodded and continued eating. "That was a really good meeting we had this afternoon," he said. "I think Persimmon Homes are going to be really interested in the land I'm going to buy."

He waited for her reply. She looked at him and knew she had to answer him. "Yes, it was a good meeting, and I think they were interested in your new project."

He smiled at her. She wanted to finish the tea quickly and go back to work. The sooner she finished, the sooner she would be back home.

Chapter 23

Lisa sat sprawled on the sofa smoking a cigarette and watching the children playing in the garden with the dog. David was down in the village pub watching a game of football. She wondered if she should have gone up to see her father and have a swim in the pool. The water was rather on the cool side, so she must mention that he had to fix it.

She knew Nancy liked to swim, and wondered how often. Nothing she had done to hurt her had worked, although she had been pretty ill after David's party. Surely she must guess that someone was trying to poison her, and she probably knew it was Lisa.

Her father had mentioned that Nancy suspected that somebody was trying to get rid of her by poisoning her. Lisa had laughed at him, and told him it was probably Nancy's imagination. The only person who knew about this was Joe, and could she really trust him? He was good at doing what she asked him to do. Her mother drifted in a dream world, and was happy to be with Joe. Joe was a good lover; otherwise her mother would have thrown him out.

Lisa was cross with Joe for telling Doris what she planned to do, and she would have to work fast, as Nancy would soon be leaving. Lisa wondered where she was moving to, probably another firm dealing with land etc, but the sooner she left her father's employment the better things would be.

Would she try it on the next secretary her father employed? She would have to see how attractive the woman turned out to be, and if her father took a fancy to her. The other secretaries her father had had were good at the work, but her father had never made any attempt to have a social life with them. Nancy was an attractive woman, in her forties and single, but she was probably not looking for romance, at least not with Gordon. Her father was quite boring; when she had been a child he had been more interested in making money than playing with his daughter. Perhaps that was why she had more in common with her mother, although Lisa was allowed to please herself, as her mother was never really strict with her.

She reached for the phone to ring Joe. She put out her cigarette and dialled the number.

"Hi Joe, it's me. How are you doing?"

He sounded sleepy. "Oh hi Lisa, what have you been up to? Nancy will be going in a couple of weeks, have you got any plans?" He wiped the sleep from his eyes and sat up.

This was Saturday and Doris was away shopping for new clothes.

"Is mother in, or is she out shopping?" asked Lisa.

Joe felt safe to talk without her mother hovering in the background. "Yes, Doris is away shopping, as usual on a Saturday," said Joe. He drew a cigarette from the packet, lit it and inhaled. Then he lay back on the pillow and waited for her to speak.

"Joe, this is what I've planned. Nancy finishes work around 5 pm, gets into her car and drives home, unless she stays for supper with Dad. We will have to give her a small drug to make her sleep, and then we'll put her upstairs in the small room. It depends how long she will sleep for, and how much drug we give her. She could be there for two days or more before the next plan," said Lisa, putting her cigarette out.

"Oh lord, do you think this is going to work? Your father could become suspicious."

"You bet it's going to work, I just want her to remember what a good time she had working here for Dad. I'm not going to kill her, just a way of saying farewell." She laughed. "So Joe are you in or out." She waited to hear his reply. Joe took a drag on his cigarette and thought that this could be exciting and yet, if they were caught, he could be sacked.

Sam was a quiet bloke who never really gossiped and got on with the work in hand. He wondered if Sam was gay. He would have to make sure that Gordon and Sam were out of house and office, so they did not know what was happening. He said, "Look, what about Sam and your father. We would have to make sure they were far away. Sam works late sometimes, which could make things difficult."

"You stop worrying about Sam and my father; I'll take care of it. We will make it a couple of days before the Friday she leaves, but I'll take her out of that room and suggest a swim in the pool. What do you think?" she said.

There was silence for a minute.

"Are you there Joe, you haven't answered me? For god's sake stop worrying it will work out honest."

"Yes, I'm here. Okay, you're on. Pity we are doing this to her, she really is a nice woman." He put his cigarette out.

"Oh, for goodness sake Joe, you sound as though you're in love with her." This was not what she wanted Joe to say at a time like this, while they were making plans. "Have you fallen for her?"

"No, of course not. Look, Doris is coming in, I'll talk with you soon." He put the phone down, smiling at Doris, who was coming into the room loaded with shopping bags.

"Look what I've bought, want to see?" said Doris, coming over to him. She kissed him and sat down beside him. He smiled at her and took her in his arms and kissed her. "Wonderful, you're going to look smashing tonight."

"Why, where are we going, somewhere special?" she said, kissing him on the cheek.

"Where would like to go, my love?" he said, pulling out another cigarette.

"The town was heaving with folk, as well as the usual visitors," said Doris, taking his cigarette from him and drawing from it. Joe scratched his chin; he needed a shave. He took the cigarette from her and said "Lisa was on the phone a short while ago, she was wondering if she should go and visit her dad and have a swim in the pool."

Doris started packing away her new clothes. "Lisa, oh yes, of course, she's very fond of her father, and she visits him more than she comes here. I'm not jealous or anything, but he's loaded, he can take care of her."

Joe laughed, got up and went towards the bathroom. He said, "I am going to have a shave, why don't you wear that little black number tonight. You look good in it."

Doris shook her head and giggled. She packed the clothes in the wardrobe and went and made herself a cup of coffee.

Gordon decided that as it was Saturday, he would phone Nancy and ask her out for dinner. That should cheer her up, as she had seemed so depressed yesterday. Maybe he had been too hard on her squeezing her arm like that, but she did not seem to be all that interested.

The phone rang out. He waited for a few minutes, and then put it down. It suddenly rang, and he lifted it up, hoping that he would be speaking to Nancy.

"Hello Dad, it's Lisa. Are you doing anything special at

the moment?" she asked. There was silence for a second and then he replied, "Hello dear, how are you and the children doing?" He wondered what she was phoning for.

"Oh, I wondered if I could come up with the kids and have a quick swim in the pool. You know Dad, you should do something with the water, as the temperature is darn cool. Just try and make it warmer. Can you do that, or do you have to get a mechanic to fix it?"

Gordon thought for a moment. He was not doing anything except thinking of Nancy. He replied, "What time are you coming up? I have to fix the water and it could take a wee while."

Lisa shrugged. By the time she made to East Lothian, it would be time to come home. "Forget it Dad. I'll come tomorrow at eleven with the kids, if that's okay," she said.

Gordon looked at his watch and replied. "Yes, that will be okay, and I'll get some nice cake and refreshments for you and the children."

"Great Dad, see you tomorrow. Bye."

Nancy had stood looking at the phone until it rang out. She hoped Bob would have phoned her, but just in case it was Gordon she did not answer it. She checked the number, and it was indeed Gordon. She wondered what he wanted, perhaps he was going to apologise for his behaviour yesterday. She sat down and sipped her tea. Now she was going to be frightened every time the phone went, just In case it was Gordon. *Pull yourself together, and try not to be so silly,* she told herself. She would phone Bob, so that Gordon would not able to phone her.

Bob answered straight away. "Hello honey, how are you?" he asked.

Nancy gave a sigh of relief. "The phone rang earlier on and I didn't answer it, because it was Gordon," she said. "I am afraid of what he is going to say to me. Yesterday, we went to view some land he thought of buying, and asked me for my opinion. I could not give him one, and gave a negative answer, and before going to the car he gripped my arm and squeezed it very hard, which really hurt me."

"Did you shout out, so that he would know? It really looks like he is taking it out on you because you are leaving. How long have you got to go?"

"Another two weeks, and I'm wondering how I'm ever going to last out. I have this awful feeling something is going to happen to me, and I'm beginning to get scared." She twisted her hands together.

"Oh my dear, try to stop worrying, perhaps nothing will happen. You'll probably get a clock, a bunch of flowers and a goodbye. Look, I'll take you out tonight and we'll forget all your troubles and enjoy ourselves," said Bob, trying to calm her.

Nancy pulled herself together and said, "Yes, thank you for calming me down, I'll look forward to going out and enjoying myself. See you at seven."

"Stop worrying, enjoy your weekend and try not to think of work or the Mackenzie family. Chin up, I'll see you later," said Bob, blowing kisses down the phone.

Nancy was relieved, as Bob always calmed her; she knew she was worrying unnecessarily. She went to the bedroom and took an outfit out, spread it on the bed, and made her way to the bathroom to get ready.

Chapter 24

Nancy continued to work her time as the days slowly went by. One day she noticed a tall woman who had turned up for an interview. She looked to be in her thirties, with her hair pulled neatly into a tight bun. Nancy kept her fingers crossed, hoping that she would not have to show the woman what to do. She gathered that she was from a secretarial agency.

She heard voices, and Gordon ushered the woman into the small study for her interview. Nancy kept trying to listen to the conversation, which was hard to hear from her room. She noticed that Sam was coming over with some files. She wondered if it was an excuse to talk to her. He knocked on the door and entered.

"Morning Nancy, just brought some more stuff to be filed away in the cabinet," he said.

She smiled at him, and took the files. "I not going to ask how you're doing over there, as I'm forever asking you that."

He laughed. "Not long now and you'll be leaving us. I hope you've found a suitable post to go to. I'll miss you Nancy, as you've been a friend. I hope the office you will be going to will appreciate you." He blushed as he was speaking. She felt quite tearful, realising he was wishing her well. She got up and came round to give him a hug, feeling rather embarrassed. Sam blushed and cleared his throat and said, "Well, I'd better be off back to work. I wish you all the very best." He left before she could say anything else.

She hoped Joe would not be coming over to wish her well and get another kiss. She was relieved when that did not happen.

Later on Gordon came through with the woman who had had the interview. She looked young and quite attractive. He said to Nancy. "This is Miss Grenfell, she will start work in a few weeks time."

The woman smiled at Nancy and stuck out her hand for the introduction. "Nice to meet you," said Nancy. The woman smiled nervously and looked at Gordon.

Nancy sat down, wondering what he was going to say next. He took Miss Grenfell by the elbow and then disappeared, probably for the usual cup of coffee. Nancy thought, good luck to you dear, I hope you will be very happy working for him. She wondered if Miss Grenfell would have the tour of the house, and if she could swim. She wondered if she would get a farewell party with some gifts. and good wishes for her future. She somehow did not think so.

There was a meeting in the afternoon with Persimmon Homes. Nancy as usual got the room ready for the meeting. She made tea and coffee and poured them into heated jugs, along with some chocolate biscuits. This could be the last meeting she would take, as she spread the files out in front of Gordon's chair. She was not sure how many people would turn up, but there were usually four to six men.

Gordon did not invite Nancy for lunch. Instead he went away to have lunch with Miss Grenfell at a hotel in North Berwick or Haddington.

The meeting took place at 2pm and three men from Persimmon Homes turned up. Everyone seemed to be in a good mood, with the men laughing at some joke Gordon had made. Nancy did not think it was funny, but she smiled and waited for Gordon to start the meeting. It went well and he seemed to be on his best behaviour. They came to some arrangement that phase one would go ahead. Gordon disappeared with two of the chaps, while a Mr Rossi stayed back. He said to Nancy. "I hear you're leaving Mr Mackenzie's employment quite soon."

Nancy looked at him and wondered if everyone in the house-building business knew she was leaving. "Yes, I'll be leaving next week, and am joining Taylor Wimpey employment in a few weeks time," she said.

He smiled at her. "I didn't know you were going to work for Taylor Wimpey, if I had known we could have offered you a post with our company. Pity, but there it is." He squeezed her arm. Nancy just smiled at him. Nancy wasn't going to mention that Persimmon Homes had invited her to work for them, as that would really stick in Gordon's throat.

Joe sat back in his chair and said to Sam, who was busy working, "Well, did you see the new secretary? Quite a looker, and younger than Nancy."

"Nothing to do with us," said Sam, not looking up. "She probably won't have the experience that Nancy has."

Joe laughed and teased Sam by saying, "Sam fancies Nancy."

Sam blushed and put his head down and got on with the work. Joe laughed and spun around in his seat. "I bet Gordon took her out for lunch, he usually does when he interviews a new secretary." He took a drag on his cigarette.

Sam was slowly getting annoyed with Joe and his tittle-tattle about women, which did not interest him.

Nancy had to type out the documents for Phase One that Gordon had accepted, as they had to be sent out and signed by Persimmon Homes. She sat and wondered how she really felt, as that had been her very last meeting. She had not seen Gordon since the meeting, and knew he would be relaxing in the conservatory smoking his cigars. She took her time in typing out the documents, and hoped that when she finished she could go home and telephone Bob.

At four o' clock, Gordon appeared in the doorway, and

said to her. "Thanks Nancy for typing up these documents so quickly. The meeting was really good, I thought."

"Yes, it went very well indeed and everyone was in such a good mood," she replied. What was she supposed to say? Obviously, he was in a good mood. She hoped he was not going to ask her to stay over for supper.

"Come and have some tea with me in the conservatory," he said, and walked away. Nancy felt like a naughty school girl, getting permission to leave the room. What could they possibly talk about? She sat as far away as possible from him, and waited for him to start the conversation.

He placed his mug down on the mat and looked at her. He was comparing her with the new lady, Miss Grenfell, and wondered if he felt the same way as he had done with Nancy.

"Miss Grenfell seems to be well educated and her qualifications are very good," he said. Nancy thought, do I really want to hear about this new woman?

"Oh good, I'm sure she'll make a marvellous secretary," she said. He raised an eyebrow, surprised at her reply.

"I'm sure she will be good, I do hope so" he said, sipping his tea and glancing over at Nancy.

The phone started ringing, and Gordon answered it. He spoke in quiet tones; whoever it was; he probably did want her to hear his conversation. Nancy finished her tea, got up and tiptoed out of the room, glad to be able to finish off the documents.

Nancy was glad when she reached home, as she felt the whole day had been a bit of a strain, and hoped that her last week would go quickly and smoothly.

Chapter 25

Lisa rummaged in the large box she had taken down from the attic and took out a box of tablets. She shook the box, opened it and counted how many there were. David shouted up to her regarding the children, who were arguing, and she pushed the ladder back up into the attic. What now she wondered, could he not control the children? She stood at the top of stairs shielding the box behind her back, so that David could not see what she had. He stood looking up at her.

"Are you coming down or what?" he said. She took the stairs down towards him and said,

"What's wrong with you, can you not control your kids? Do I have to do everything?"

She walked past him and went into the lounge, where she it up a cigarette. She had to contact Joe, as time was moving fast, and Nancy would be leaving in a few days' time.

"Why don't you take the children to the beach since its Sunday," she said, turning to look at him. He stood gazing at her and shrugged. He lifted his jacket off the hall stand and placed it over his arm.

"What are you doing? Will you be coming with us?" he asked.

She looked at him and drew on her cigarette. "No, I have something to do. It will do you and the kids good to get some fresh air, and take the dog."

David shrugged, called the dog and the kids and vanished out of the door.

Lisa sighed and sat down on the couch. There was so much to do and so many things to work out. She reached for the phone and dialled Joe's number. After three rings the phone was answered.

"Hi Joe, it's Lisa. Now we have to make a plan, as Nancy will be leaving soon. Have you any ideas?"

"I thought you had all the ideas" he said, lighting up a cigarette.

"You always leave everything to me. Come on, what can you suggest?" she asked, placing her legs on the footstool. Men were hopeless in making plans, they depended on women to dictate what they want. Was he like that with her mother? Did she make all the arrangements?

Joe wiped his mouth and took a drag from his cigarette. "No, I'm thinking that after we've put the tablets in her coffee and taken her upstairs to the wee room, we have to perhaps wake her up, in case she sleeps for days on end."

Lisa shook her head and replied, "Joe, she will not sleep for days on end, because we have to get her up and take her to the swimming pool for the final goodbye."

He laughed and replied, "Are you sure you want to go ahead with this? It could be dangerous. She may never wake up."

Lisa smiled. If she died, so what? The police would turn up and she would say that Nancy had had a heart attack, and no blame would be placed on her or Joe. If her plans did work out and both of them were in the water, what if Nancy died by drowning? What would her father say or do? She had to concentrate, as this plan could not fail.

"Joe, this plan will work, believe me it will. Now we have to arrange the day when we can go ahead and do it."

Joe sat up and flicked the ash into the full ashtray. "There's another woman starting in a few weeks' time. She's younger than Nancy and good looking" he said, chuckling to himself.

Lisa raised her eyes and shook her head. He had to stop thinking of women and concentrate on this business. What was wrong with him?

"Now stop and listen. This is what's going to happen. Nancy will be working as usual in her room, and later in the afternoon, we'll give her a cup of coffee or tea plus a biscuit and put some tablets in it. It will probably take a while to work. We'll make sure that Sam and father are away out on a business trip, you can arrange that. When she falls asleep, you carry her up to the wee room and put her on the bed."

"What about her car? It'll be on the driveway. We'll have to remove it and hide it somewhere."

Lisa lit another cigarette and said, "Well, that's your job to do, you can take it somewhere, but be careful not where it will be stolen."

Joe sighed and pushed back his hair. "Okay, I'll do it. How are you going to get her to the swimming pool? Am I carrying her or will she be walking?" He leaned back on the sofa, letting the smoke rise to the ceiling.

"I'll change her into a bathing costume, and she'll be fully awake, perhaps a little drowsy," Lisa said. She got up and switched the television on. The family would be back soon and no doubt hungry.

"The best time to do this will be the day before she actually leaves," said Joe.

"Right, you're on. Make it Thursday afternoon, in case she's asleep for twenty-four hours. I'll go and see father the day before, and the next day you can make sure father and Sam are away from the house and the office."

Joe rubbed his hands together at the thought of kidnapping. Nancy. Could she swim, and what was Lisa going to do with her in the water? He knew Lisa disliked her, but to go as far as this was really quite dangerous. He really hoped it was going to work out.

Chapter 26

Nancy sat opposite Bob in the café where they were having a coffee and cake. She looked across at him and wondered if this would be the last time she was with him. She dreaded going back to work the next day, and had an awful feeling that something was going to happen to her.

"I'm finding it hard to relax this weekend," she said. "I keep thinking of going to work tomorrow, and on my last day, I was beginning to wonder if Gordon would give me a bouquet of flowers and the usual clock." She laughed, and Bob laughed as well. He took hold of her hands and gave them a friendly squeeze.

"You're going to be fine, and I'm sure Gordon will give you a nice present and perhaps a kiss to wish you on your way," he said.

She knew he was teasing her, and she felt tears in her eyes. She could not cry here in front of all these people. She looked out of the window at people floating past.

"Hey, a penny for your thoughts" said Bob, giving her hands another squeeze. She looked at him and smiled. "Seriously, I have this feeling that I may die next Friday."

Bob looked at her in horror. "Come on now, you told me you had a nightmare, with Lisa, Joe and Gordon chasing you. It was only a bad dream." He drank the rest of his coffee and stood up. "Let's go for a long walk and get some fresh air, it's a beautiful day." She put on her jacket and drank the rest of her coffee, and they both walked out.

Bob knew that Nancy was scared, and perhaps had a premonition that something was going to happen to her. He had to keep her spirits up and not mention work. He held her hand and they walked through the meadows, enjoying the scenery of nature. He thought he would cook a nice meal with a nice bottle of wine, and that would cheer her up. Nancy was grateful that Bob was being kind and cheerful, and indeed she forgot all about Gordon and work.

Nancy returned home quite late, and she put the kettle on for a cup of tea. She had got a taxi home as she did not want to wait for a bus, as one could wait for over half an hour for one to come along. She changed into her night clothes, and sat on the couch in the lounge sipping her tea. Bob was so wonderful in keeping her spirits up and trying to keep her happy. She wondered if he was also getting worried about her leaving Gordon's employment. No, she must not keep thinking about what might happen next week.

The phone rang, and she hoped it was not Gordon.

"Hello," she said.

"Hi there, I hope you got home safely. I hope you enjoyed the weekend as much as I did," said Bob. He gave a little laugh.

"Yes. I've had a wonderful weekend, and am sorry for being such an annoying person going on about work," she replied. "Thanks for phoning, and wishing me good night. I love you." It was true; she did love Bob.

"I love you too honey. Sleep well and I'll phone you tomorrow," he said, blowing a kiss down the phone.

The next day Nancy took her time in driving all the way to East Lothian; thank god it would be nearly the last time she would have to drive over this week. There were three cars in the car park, and Nancy wondered if Miss Grenfell was starting work. She went to her room and sat down. She glanced out of the window and saw Sam and Joe getting into a car and driving off somewhere. She heard voices and peeped out of the doorway to see who was visiting. She could hear Gordon talking to someone, so she returned to her desk.

She flicked over a newspaper and began to read. Gordon appeared in the doorway and said, "Morning Nancy. Well, it's your last week."

"Yes, that's right. Have you anything for me to do?" she asked.

Gordon smiled. He was holding a large file in his hands; he placed it on the desk and said, "Here you are. Could you type up these documents? I need them for tomorrow."

Nancy opened the file and waited for him to depart. He said, "I'm truly sorry that you weren't happy working for me these past few weeks. I'll say it again, you're the best secretary I've ever had. I'll miss you and I hope we'll stay friends."

Nancy sat and looked at him. What could she say? She was leaving and that was that. She swallowed. "I've enjoyed working for you Gordon, but I feel that I must move on with my life and think of my future."

He stared at her and wondered if that was all she was going to say. No words to say "thank you Gordon, for all you did for me". He stood watching her, and she started to fidget with the file. Why could he not just go away and leave her to get on? What else could she say? "I'm glad to be leaving you and your awful family"?

He left the room, and she gave a sigh of relief that he had gone. Was he going to start reminiscing about the relationship she had had with him?

Later on that afternoon when Nancy had finished typing the documents, Gordon appeared.

"Nancy, would you come to dinner with me tonight, seeing that it's your last week? I'll understand if you don't wish to." He stood at the door looking at her. She was taken by surprise at his invitation, and wondered whether she should accept; after all, it was not often an employer asked one out on their last week."

She smiled at him. "Thank you Gordon for your kind invitation, I'll join you for dinner."

"Great, we'll go earlier so that you can get home to Edinburgh in good time."

He disappeared and she looked down at her outfit. Was it suitable for dining out? She phoned Bob; no answer, so she left a message. "Hi Bob, Gordon has asked me out to dinner tonight, and I thought I'd better accept, seeing it's my last week. I should be home by ten in case you want to phone me."

She wondered where Gordon was taking her for the meal, as she had her car parked outside. If she left it and went in his car, how was she going to drive home?

Gordon took his sports car and they set off; they did not drive to North Berwick or Haddington, but headed east. They did not speak as they travelled along, and Nancy wondered how far they were going to go. They arrived at the village of Aberlady, on the coast, where he had made reservations for dinner at the hotel for six thirty.

First they took a walk along the coastal path. It was good to get some fresh air, although there was a cool breeze from the sea. Nancy pulled her coat closer to her body as they walked along the path.

Gordon spoke. "It's not often I get out to the coast and walk with a lovely lady," he said. He looked sideways to see her reaction. She wondered what this sweet talk was leading to. She said, "Yes, it's lovely here looking at the birds flying round, and so peaceful".

As she leaned on the wooden rail of a bridge, he put an arm around her shoulders and said, "Are you cold my dear? Let's head back to the hotel and have something to eat and drink."

They were seated in a cosy corner near the fireplace where a wood stove was burning. Nancy was hungry, as she had not stopped working for lunch. The menu looked inviting and she had some soup with hot white rolls before tucking into roast lamb and trimmings. Gordon did most of the talking, mainly about how exciting it was going to be with the different companies all eager to buy his land. Time moved on and she was grateful that he was making the conversation, as she began to wonder where this was all leading to.

Gordon noticed that Nancy was very quiet and hardly said a word all evening. Perhaps she was beginning to regret that she was leaving his employment. She used to be so chatty when he took her out all those months ago, and now she hardly spoke.

Nancy was glad when they returned to Gordon's; she noted the time and it was nine thirty. Getting out of the car Gordon said, "Come in for a coffee before you go, as we both had wine at dinner."

Nancy paused. She wanted to get home and she was

certainly not going to stay over. But she thought maybe he was right, so she said, closing the car door, "Okay, just a quick cup, then I must go." She followed him into the house and went to the kitchen, where he put the kettle on. He fiddled with mugs and opened a packet of biscuits, placing them on a plate. She felt like a stranger on a first date, with this man that allowed him to hug and kiss her months ago. She leaned against a cabinet, watching him.

"Is there anything the matter Nancy, you're very quiet? Are you feeling unwell?" he asked, looking at her. Nancy looked down at her feet. What could she say – that she wanted to leave him and the work and be herself again?

"I'm just a bit tired, that's all," she said. She noticed that he had poured a small liqueur into a glass. Was he trying to make her drunk so she could not go home? She followed him upstairs to the lounge and sat on an armchair, so she would not be sitting beside him. He poured out the coffee and placed it on a table beside her.

"Now, Nancy my dear" he said, stirring his coffee and sitting looking at her. She sipped the coffee. "I'm sure you'll be looking forward to your new secretary starting soon," she said. She wondered why she had said that.

He stared at her for a moment before speaking, "Are you having doubts about leaving me, Nancy?" he said.

She had not meant to say that, but before she knew it he was over and kissing her on the lips. He was practically sitting on her lap. He lifted her off her seat taking her in his arms and kissing her again. She should have known something like this was going to happen. That was the reason he had asked her out for dinner so he could try and win her love back.

She pushed him away and said, "Gordon, you cannot do this to me. I like you, but I don't love you." He stood looking shocked and amazed and said, "Somehow you've changed. Perhaps the work's becoming boring, and I had no time for romance. You're probably dating someone else, you are aren't you?" He was almost crying. Nancy did not know what to do. She did not realise that he had really loved her, and she must have given the impression that she loved him also.

"I am so sorry I gave you the impression that I was in love with you," she said. "I like you a lot, but I can't love you the way you want me to. I am dating someone and have been for a good while." She stood there helpless looking at him. Thank god she was leaving at the end of the week; she could not continue working under these awful circumstances. "I have to go home now. But thank you Gordon for taking me out for dinner." She reached for her coat and bag. He was still looking as if he could not take in what she had said. She came over and kissed him on the cheek, giving his arm a squeeze.

"I'll see you tomorrow," she said. She left him in the middle of the room, and quietly went downstairs and got into her car. She stood and took a deep breath glancing around her, at the house and the annexe where the men worked. She slipped into the car and drove off down the avenue.

Chapter 27

Joe arrived at Lisa's late the following afternoon to arrange the final items that would be needed to give to Nancy before she was taken to the secret room. They needed to work fast as the evening was drawing near. Lisa showed Joe a syringe, which she would give Nancy as the dose to make her sleep for some hours. Joe wanted to know what Lisa had intended to do at the swimming pool. He knew Nancy was a swimmer, and anything that Lisa had intended to do, Nancy would survive.

Lisa looked at Joe and said, "Relax, I've got everything in hand, all you have to do is get father and Sam out of the house for a few hours on the Friday." Joe rubbed his face and said, "What will happen on the Thursday, after we have Nancy in the secret room? Gordon may wonder where Nancy is, as he might invite her for a meal at the house."

"Oh for god's sake, now you're starting to panic. If I

knew you were getting panicky, I wouldn't have asked you to help me. I need you to carry her up to the room, as I can't do it. Here is a small bag that you can take with you, as David might wonder why I was packing up a bag." She handed him a small bag, which contained the syringe and bathing costumes. She said to him. "By the way can you swim? Just in case Nancy tries to drown me?" He looked at her. "Yes, of course I can. Am I supposed to be in the water at the same time as you?"

"No, you'll have to keep watch in case father and Sam return early. You can do that, can't you?" She slammed the drawers to a cabinet shut. He made his way down the stairs, and turned around as she came up to him.

"Well the best of luck, as we're going to need it. I'll leave the bag in the boot of the car. I don't think Sam drives the car, as we always use mine when we have to go anywhere. What time on Thursday will we give her the injection?"

Lisa rubbed her eyes. "Before she leaves to go home you will have to get rid of her car, so that it looks like she has gone home already. I'll be visiting Dad and I'll keep him occupied when you take her upstairs. Before you take her up I'll give her the injection, which I'll do in her room. Don't worry. I'll see you tomorrow. Try and think up some excuse to get Dad and Sam away somewhere far away from the house. Please don't tell mother about this, because she'll tell Dad and then our little escapade will fail."

She stepped forward and kissed him on the cheek, then opened the door and shooed him out.

Lisa looked at the clock on the wall and, made her way to the kitchen, as she knew David would be picking the children up from school. She took the phone and dialled Gordon's number. Gordon picked it up.

"Hello Lisa, how are you today?" he said. "Children okay, and that husband of yours?" He drew on the cigar he had just lit up.

Lisa laughed. "Tomorrow is Thursday, I wonder if it's okay to come and see you in the afternoon? I know it's a working day, and Nancy will be leaving on Friday. Are you giving her a farewell present?" She waited to hear what he had to say.

He puffed smoke out towards the ceiling, looking at two cats sunbathing on the wall. He thought, of course, Nancy was leaving tomorrow. Did she deserve a present? She had been quite rude the other evening after dinner. He said, "Yes, I'll give her a present, have you any ideas?"

Lisa gave a little laugh. She knew what Nancy deserved to get and she would be getting that on Friday. She said, "Oh Dad, you know, a bunch of flowers and a clock, that's the usual thing to give employees when they leave."

Gordon laughed and replied, "Very funny. You know I have a new lady starting in two weeks' time, I'm sure she will do well as my new secretary."

Lisa giggled. "A new secretary. Goodness me, you do go through them. What's this woman like, young or old?"

Gordon wondered if Lisa was making jokes. "Younger than Nancy, she's a Miss Grenfell. Why are you so interested? About tomorrow, yes do come up later on in the afternoon. You can say good bye to Nancy."

Lisa thought that would be about right. "I have to go now as the kids and David have just returned, See you tomorrow, Dad."

"Good bye darling see you tomorrow." Gordon finished his cigar and made his way to the kitchen, where he poured himself a glass of wine.

Chapter 28

Nancy woke up early on Thursday morning and looked at the clock, which read six o'clock. She dreaded going to work at Gordon's, and tomorrow was her last day. She knew she did not have to start work at Taylor Wimpey for another two weeks, which gave her time to relax and start fresh.

She wondered if her romance with Bob would last, as their relationship might stop if his wife wanted him back. She still missed Christopher after all the years they had been married, and after being on her own for such a long time, she wondered if she would ever get married again.

She got out of bed and went to the kitchen to put the kettle on before going to the bathroom. She wondered what she would wear; of course, that depended on the weather. She placed a garment on the bed, took a few dresses out of the wardrobe and decided she would wear the blue dress. She took her time over breakfast listening to the news on the television. She would be over to East Lothian slightly later then she should be, but who cared if she was late and Gordon got worried that she might not turn up. She wondered if he was going to be nice to her, and not make remarks about her leaving him.

She arrived at Gordon's and went to her room. There was nothing on her desk, and she sat looking out of the window. The building seemed to be silent, and she wondered if she was alone, and where were Gordon, Sam and Joe.

She took a newspaper out of her bag and started to read it. Was Gordon expecting her into work today, and where was he? She heard a door slam and then footsteps as if someone was coming down the stairs. She hurriedly removed the paper and pretended to look for something in her bag. Gordon appeared, looking tired and worried, as if he had not slept all night.

"Ah, there you are Nancy" he said, looking in at her from the doorway.

She lifted her head and said, "Yes, here I am."

He looked at his watch and then at her and said, "Come and have some coffee in the conservatory. I slept in today, and I haven't had any breakfast."

She followed him into the kitchen, where he had switched the kettle on. He fussed about placing mugs on a tray, and poured cereal into a bowl, drowning it with milk. He took a banana and placed that on the tray. When the kettle had boiled he put coffee into the mugs, and poured the water on the coffee. Nobody had spoken while this performance was going on; Nancy just stood looking at his antics.

She followed him in to the conservatory, where he placed his breakfast on a table. She took her coffee and sat down facing him. He peeled his banana, put it on top of his cereal and greedily started eating. "Gosh, I never thought I would be so hungry," he said, munching away. Nancy did not say anything; she continued to drink her coffee, watching him eating. He looked at her and thought she looked rather pale. Perhaps she was having second thoughts about leaving.

"Are you all right? You look rather pale my dear," he said, finishing his cereal.

She smiled. "No, I'm just a bit tired, that's all." She finished her coffee and put her mug on the table.

"Now my dear, I think we should go for a drive and have some lunch out. That will cheer you up." He wiped his mouth with the back of his hand. Nancy was all for that, because to stay there with him and do nothing would be very boring. She replied, "Yes, that would be nice thank you." It would soon be lunchtime. She wondered where he was going to take her. Hopefully he would behave himself this time and not try to kiss her.

"Right, I'm going to make a few phone calls, why don't you relax in here," he said, lifting the tray and disappearing into the kitchen. Nancy got up and glanced out at the garden. She sat down and closed her eyes. She did feel tired, and perhaps she could have a sleep.

Some time later, she woke with a jump and sat up straight as Gordon appeared.

"Right, are you ready? Get your coat and bag and we'll be off."

Once again they went in his sports car. He drove far too fast and she wondered if he got any speeding tickets. She did not speak, as she did not want to disturb his concentration while driving. Eventually, they arrived in Haddington and went to a bistro by a river. He had booked a table, and they sat by a window which looked out at a small garden. The menu looked interesting and Nancy was hungry, as it was a long time since she had had breakfast.

After lunch, he drove along a road and turned into a large driveway where a house stood. He got out of the car and Nancy saw Ursula standing in the doorway smiling at them. Nancy wondered if this was a goodbye for her sake, as she probably would not be seeing the sisters ever again.

Gordon kissed his sister on the cheek and ushered Nancy forward.

"Oh lovely to see you both. Come on in," said Ursula, standing back to let them through. They were ushered into a large lounge with big bay windows looking out on to the drive. Heavy curtains hung neatly down to the floor, and a vase of roses stood on a table. Nancy sat down on the sofa and waited to see what would happen next.

"We've had lunch, so don't make a fuss regarding tea etc," said Gordon, sitting in the nearest chair. Ursula looked at Nancy. "I'm sure you would like a cup of tea. I made some scones and teacakes, you have to have some." She looked at her brother. Gordon shrugged. "Okay, we'll have some tea as you have obviously been busy," he said, sitting back in his chair.

Nancy looked around the room. There was a large mirror over the mantelpiece, and she could see that Ursula liked antique furniture. Ursula came in, pulling a trolley full of sandwiches, scones and cakes. Nancy was told to help herself to the food, and she put some sandwiches on her plate. The tea was very weak, and was probably mint tea or green tea. They made polite conversation, and Nancy wondered why she had been invited to his sister's house.

After a time, Gordon excused himself and went out of the room. Ursula came and sat down beside Nancy. She placed a hand on top of Nancy's and said, "My dear, it must be soon that you are leaving Gordon's employment and going onto other adventures. You know I'll miss you, as I've heard you are an excellent worker."

Nancy wondered what she could say. She took her hand from under Ursula's, and replied, "I know it's been hard for Gordon and I've found it difficult to leave, but life must go on, and I cannot always be working for Gordon. I have a life to lead, and since my husband passed away some years ago, I feel I have to move on and get on with my life."

Ursula patted her hand. "Of course you do, why on earth would you want to stay with Gordon? Unless, of course, he has proposed marriage to you." She raised an eyebrow. Nancy understood why Gordon had left the two women to talk.

Nancy said, "No, he has not proposed marriage to me, and I am afraid I feel I could not accept such a proposal. I am fond of him, but not in a romantic way. So if you were hoping for a wedding, I am sorry to disappoint you."

Ursula stood up and looked out the window, then turned and said, "Of course my dear, it's just that you have been like a friend to all of us, and we will miss you."

Gordon came through the door and picked up his coat. He looked at Nancy and said, "Ready to go. Thank you dear for a lovely tea. Give my love to Jean and company."

Nancy stood up and shook hands with Ursula, who planted a kiss on her cheek. Nancy waved good bye to her as the car drove out of the driveway.

Chapter 29

After visiting Ursula, they returned to Greenlands. As there did not seem to be any work for her to do, Nancy thought she might be able to go home. She sat in the conservatory, gazing out of the window, while Gordon pottered about in the kitchen. She did not want another cup of tea or anything to eat.

She heard voices and saw Lisa approaching. Nancy began to panic; she did not want to meet Lisa and she certainly did not want to accept any drinks from her.

"Hello Dad, where are you?" enquired Lisa, going into the kitchen. She greeted her father with a kiss on the cheek. He was putting away plates and cups from the morning coffee and breakfast.

"Hello dear," he said, wiping his hands. "I was going to make a cup of tea with some cake and biscuits. Did you bring the children?"

Lisa shook her head. "No. I said I would come and see you. David's looking after them." She hoped Joe had got the room upstairs ready for Nancy, and felt in her bag for the syringe. She smiled to herself. It was convenient that Nancy was still here.

Nancy tiptoed out of the conservatory, and made for her room while Lisa was still talking to her father. She hoped to get her coat and bag ready to make a dash for the car. She heard Gordon calling her and paused, wondering what to do. She put down her coat and bag and came to the conservatory door. Gordon was issuing plates, and started pouring out the tea. "Come and have some tea before you go home" he said, looking up at her.

Nancy looked at Lisa, who stood smiling coldly at her. Nancy did not like the look Lisa was giving her, but she sat down in the nearest chair and took the cup of tea Gordon had handed to her. She took a biscuit, and sat looking at them. Gordon sat down, stirring his tea.

"Well Nancy, it's your last day tomorrow. I do hope you'll enjoy working for the new company. I've not mentioned any names, as that is not fair for you and other people who have nothing to do with you to hear where you will be going. By the way, I'll need your car for Miss Grenfell, so tomorrow could you get a lift home please."

Lisa just sat and smiled. Nancy wondered why she was grinning so much. What was she up to? She looked at the tea in her cup and wondered if Lisa had put anything in it.

She tried to relax and said to Gordon, "Yes of course, I'll leave the car for Miss Grenfell. I hope she'll be very happy working for you."

Gordon smiled and passed the cakes around the company. Nancy shook her head as she watched Lisa stuffing her face with cake. She hated this small talk that they were making, as she just wanted to be away from the house and both of them. She glanced at the clock on the mantelpiece, which said five o'clock. She did not want to be rude, but she was terrified that Gordon was going to suggest supper.

Lisa watched every movement Nancy made, and wondered how she was going to inject her with the sleeping draught.

The phone went and Gordon picked up it up. "Hello Joe. Yes, what's that? Oh dear, OK I'll come over." He looked at the women and said. "Joe wants me to look over a document, so I'll nip over and see to it. Oh Nancy, in case I don't see you before you go, safe home and I'll see you tomorrow."

He left Nancy looking at Lisa. Nancy got up and made her way to her room. She picked up her coat and handbag, and turned to find Lisa standing behind her.

"Oh, going so soon?" said Lisa, stepping a bit nearer. Nancy looked at her, placing her coat over her arm.

"Yes, it's getting late. Thank Gordon for the tea," she said.

She walked towards Lisa, and the next thing she knew was a sudden pain in her arm. She gave a sharp cry and felt herself falling. She slumped to the floor and lay unconscious.

Lisa stepped back and looked out of the window, noticing that Nancy's car was not there, and Joe was running towards the house. He came in panting. Lisa said, "Quick, we'll take her up to the room, I'll bring her belongings before Dad comes back."

They carried Nancy up the stairs and into the bedroom, where the panel in the wall was open. Joe lifted Nancy on to the bed and placed a blanket over her. Lisa laid her coat and handbag on a chair. Lisa said to the unconscious Nancy, "Sweet dreams bitch, see you tomorrow." Joe closed over the panel and both of them ran down the stairs, as they had seen Gordon approaching the house.

Joe ducked into the bathroom, as he could hear Lisa talking to her father. Then he came out and ran over to the annexe, where he sat behind his desk. He wiped his face; that had been a close shave. He had made an excuse to Gordon about some papers he had to show him, but had left it in his car. He left Gordon studying the document and made his way to the house. He had not expected Gordon to make his way back to the house so soon, but it was clear that Lisa would keep her father talking.

After a while Gordon realised that Nancy must have returned home, so he invited Lisa to stay and have some supper with him.

Bob phoned Nancy's number once again; still no answer.

He checked the time on his watch and noted that it was after 7 pm. She should be back home by now, unless Gordon had persuaded her to stay for supper. He knew she did not want to have supper with him, as tomorrow was her last day at work.

He paced up and down the room. Surely she should be home by now? Or had something happened to her? He hardly ate his supper, and poured himself another glass of whisky to calm his nerves. He sat down at the table and glanced at his phone again. He was worried now, and tried to remember what she had said the other day in the café about what if something happened to her.

He put his hands over his face. God no, surely nothing had happened to her? Suppose Lisa had turned up at Gordon's and put something in her drink and she was lying somewhere dying? He wondered if he should phone Gordon to see if she was still there, though he did not want to have to speak to the man, as he thought he was selfish, rude and possessive.

He looked at his watch again, it was half past seven. He lifted his phone, but then changed his mind and put it back on the table. Oh Nancy, where are you? Should he phone the police? No, it was too soon for that.

After a further half hour Bob decided that he would try Nancy's number one more time, and if she still did not answer, he would phone Gordon.

The phone rang out.

He switched on the news in case there was something about a woman and an accident, but there was nothing. He lifted his phone and phoned Gordon. The phone was immediately answered.

"Hello, Gordon Mackenzie speaking," said Gordon, wondering who on earth was phoning at this time of night.

"Hello Gordon, this is Bob Jones, can I speak to Nancy?"

There was a pause before Gordon replied. "She went home just after five o'clock. Why are you phoning, is she not at home?" Bob's name seemed familiar, and Gordon suddenly realised that this must be the man who was dating her.

"Sorry to disturb you," said Bob, who was beginning to panic. "She's not answering her phone, and I wondered if she was still with you working."

"No, she's not here. God, I hope nothing has happened to her," said Gordon, beginning to feel worried himself.

"Well thanks for telling me anyway," said Bob. He put the phone down. He phoned the main hospital, in case she was there after a serious accident, but there was nothing. He was really worried now, and decided that if he had not heard from her, he would call the police the next day to report her missing.

Chapter 30

It was early morning when Nancy woke up. She looked around the room and wondered where she was. She felt drowsy, and tried to remember what exactly had happened to her.

She slowly sat up and looked over at the chair where her clothes and handbag lay. She got up, picked up her bag and looked for her phone. It was not there; somebody had taken it.

She gradually remembered what had happened. She had been going home, but Lisa was standing in her way, and then she had felt an awful pain in her arm and fallen. And then everything had gone dark.

She staggered back to the bed and lay down, still feeling very groggy. How was she going to contact Bob? He must be wondering where she was. She started to cry, but then stopped herself and wiped the tears away with the back of her hand. Why was she being punished by Gordon and Lisa? What had she done to deserve this sort of treatment? She began to wonder what they had in store for her next. Was she going to be left for another day? A week? She murmured, "Oh god help me!"

She got up and went over to the window, which looked out on to a wall or parquet of the roof. If she managed to get out, perhaps she could call for help; perhaps someone would see her. She tried to open the window, but it was stiff and would not budge. It looked too small to wriggle through, and she did not fancy wandering about the roof trying to find a way down. She gave up and returned to the small bed and pulled the blanket over her as she was feeling cold.

She was also hungry. When did she last eat? It was the afternoon tea Gordon and Lisa had made before she had tried to go home.

She drifted off back to sleep, and was awakened when someone started shaking her. She opened her eyes and looked into the face of Joe.

"Wake up, you're going for a swim" he said, shaking her again. Nancy stared up at him. He stood looking awkwardly at her. "Look, this is not my idea and I apologise for the situation you're in. This is your last day here, so let's hope you'll enjoy it."

"Why am I in this room? What are you doing with me?" said Nancy. "Somebody has taken my phone, where is it?"

Joe looked a bit startled. "Come now, get yourself into this bathing costume, but before that I'll get you some tea and toast, which will help you to wake up properly." He disappeared through the doorway, putting the panel back on the wall.

Nancy sat up and looked to see what she was wearing. She had her slip on and her dress was hanging over the chair.

After a while Joe returned with a plate of buttered toast and a mug of tea. She watched him place it on the seat of the chair, pulling it closer to her.

"Thanks" she mumbled. She attacked the toast as if she had not seen food for a long time. Joe smiled and left her eating her breakfast.

Lisa had not arrived yet, and Joe was beginning to panic. Perhaps he could let Nancy go without the ceremony that Gordon was going to give her. He had not seen his boss, and took it that he was still asleep in his bedroom. He ran downstairs and made his way down the avenue, where he had hidden Nancy's car behind an old shed. He slipped into the car and started the engine, then drove the car back up to the house, placing it where she always parked it.

Some time later, Lisa appeared, carrying a swimsuit, and made her way up to see Nancy. Time was moving fast and she wanted to get her down to the swimming pool for their swim. She met Joe on the stairs.

"Is she ready for her little swim?" she asked.

Joe looked worried. "Perhaps we should let her just go home, and forget the swim."

Lisa brushed past him. "No way is she going home after this. She'll join me for a swim, whether you like it or not."

She made her way up the stairs with Joe following her and entered the little room. She pulled up the chair, letting the plate and mug fall to the ground.

Nancy was sitting on the edge of the bed. "What are you doing? Where's my phone?" she said.

Lisa turned to Joe and said, "Is Dad up? Where is he? You'll have to make sure he's away from the house. Go on, move."

Joe looked at Nancy, then left, running down the stairs. Lisa knew she could not take Nancy down to the pool with her father in the house. She handed the swimsuit to Nancy. "Change into this, and wrap your coat around your shoulders to keep warm. I'll be back soon." She got up and ran down the stairs.

Nancy got up and walked out of the small room, looking for a bathroom. She wondered what time it was; it must be at least ten.

Joe found Gordon finishing his breakfast and said to him, "Morning Mr Mackenzie. I wanted to show you some figures, and perhaps we could go out and have a look at your land once more." He took a deep breath and waited for an answer.

Gordon looked at him and drank from his mug before

answering. "Yes all right, if you think we should have another look at it. Will Sam be joining us?"

Joe looked out of the window. He realised that Nancy's car was parked outside, and he would have to move it before Gordon saw it. "No, he's not feeling very well today, perhaps he'll be in later," he said. "I'll meet you outside in five minutes."

Joe dashed outside, got into the car and drove it away behind the annexe; there was no time to take it to the shed where it had been parked before. He was cursing Lisa for all this secrecy and for the trouble she was making.

Gordon appeared and signalled that Joe was to accompany him in the Land Rover. They made their way down the driveway, and Lisa, who was looking out of window, knew she had to make haste before they returned.

Nancy found a bathroom and took her time changing into the bathing costume; she wanted to keep Lisa waiting as long as possible. Where was Gordon? And where was Joe? He seemed to have disappeared. She could hear Lisa coming up the stairs. She looked in the mirror. Her makeup had disappeared, and she looked pale and tired. What a last day this was going to be. And how was she going to phone Bob? He must be really worried.

She saw a clock on the wall and noted that it was past eleven o'clock.

Lisa came to the entrance of the bathroom and they looked at each other.

"What's this all about, and where are you taking me now?" said Nancy.

"You're going for your farewell swim," said Lisa. She had Nancy's dress and bag over her arm and nodded for Nancy to follow her. Nancy shrugged and followed Lisa down the stairs and along the corridor towards the swimming pool. She could not understand why Lisa was doing all this.

The water looked inviting and Nancy hoped that it would be warmer than the last time she had swum. Lisa was carrying two towels and wearing a brightly coloured costume which fitted her neatly. She nodded to Nancy to encourage her to get into the water. Nancy slowly went down the steps and plunged in. She looked back to find Lisa swimming towards her.

Bob was driving as fast as he could go towards East Lothian, hoping that Nancy was still there and not lying somewhere in a ditch. He had phoned the police and told them she was missing. He also told them he was making his way to Gordon Mackenzie's house and asked them to follow.

He arrived at the same time as Gordon and Joe, who were getting out of their vehicle. He spoke to Gordon, while Joe held back. "Where is she?" asked Bob, looking at Gordon.

Gordon looked very surprised to see Bob. "Where is who, may I ask?" he said.

Bob did not answer but darted for the entrance of the house, with Gordon and Joe following him. He ran through the house and headed towards the swimming pool, where he saw Lisa and Nancy in the water. Lisa was holding Nancy's head under the water. Nancy did not seem to be moving.

"What the hell?" shouted Bob. Lisa turned and gave him an icy smile. Gordon stood at the edge with his hand over his mouth, not saying anything. Bob shoved Gordon out of the way, took off his shoes and dived into the water, then lifted Nancy in his arms and drew her towards the side. She was not moving, and her eyes were closed. He started pumping her chest and giving her the kiss of life.

Joe stood back, staring at the scene. God, had Lisa drowned her?

Gordon found his voice. "What the bloody hell are you doing?" he shouted.

"She tried to drown me, Dad," said Lisa.

"That's not how it looks from here!" he snapped.

Just then the two police officers appeared and joined the party at the poolside, One of them rushed to the poolside, ready to help Bob with Nancy. As he got there, she suddenly spluttered and started gasping for breath.

Bob looked up at Lisa. "You evil bitch, you tried to kill her!" he roared. "God knows what would have happened if I hadn't got here in time."

"No she tried to drown me, I was only defending myself," protested Lisa.

Nancy was still coughing and spluttering to remove the water from her lungs. Bob pulled her hair out of her face and looked into her eyes; she seemed OK, thank god.

"Is this your daughter sir?" said one of the officers to Gordon, indicating Lisa. He replied, "Yes, this woman is my daughter, and the other lady is my secretary, or was."

"I'll need some names please," said the officer. He took out a notebook and started writing, while his companion knelt down to check on Nancy.

Nancy gazed into Bob's face. He smiled at her and gently brushed his lips against hers. "You're all right my love, I'll look after you," he said. He gently pulled her up and placed her coat over her shoulders. Then he pointed at Lisa. "That woman is a murdering bitch," he said. "She has already tried to kill this woman several times." He helped Nancy to her feet. "Come on, we need to get you into some dry clothes."

Gordon tried to follow Bob and Nancy, who were making their way towards the house. The first officer stopped him. "We need to talk to both of you about this at the station, sir." He looked at his companion. "Get them in the car, Mike."

"Hey, what about the farewell present I was going to give her?" said Gordon.

Bob glanced round. "You can stick it up your arse for all I care," he said.

Gordon stood with his arms by his side. He shouted to Bob, "I'm sorry, I didn't know what she was up to."

Bob did not answer. As soon as he had got Nancy

dressed, he put her in the car, then drove out of the gate and headed towards Edinburgh.

★ ★ ★

Bob decided that it was best for Nancy to stay at his place, just in case Gordon turned up at her apartment. He had the keys to her flat changed, so that neither Gordon nor his family could get in.

Nancy soon recovered from her ordeal, but she would not forget it for a long time. After a few weeks, they heard that Lisa was being seen by a psychiatrist for her mental health problems, and Nancy hoped Miss Grenfell would have a happy time working for Gordon.

Nancy started work at Taylor Wimpey and was pleased to find that she was working for Mr Turner. Of course, Lisa did not have a criminal case against her, as Gordon made sure that no damage was done to the family or his business.

Dancing in the Wings

in the

A ballet story

Chapter 1

Penny Wilson was born in Edinburgh in 1947, the youngest daughter of Matthew and Margaret Wilson. Susan, their elder daughter and two years older than Penny, was training to become an actress in Glasgow. The girls were close when they were children, but after Susan went to college they each went their own way.

Penny was sixteen when she went to a local ballet school performance held in the Usher Hall in Edinburgh. They were performing "Alice in Wonderland". Penny had had some training in ballet when she was seven years of age, but gave it up when she was studying at school. After this production, she decided that she would like to train as a dancing teacher. As a student she applied to the school for the autumn term in September 1963.

Her parents had paid for their elder daughter's course in drama, but they applied to the local council for a bursary for their younger daughter to train in dance. Penny had to sit a Grade 5 exam in order to be successful. She was highly commended, and managed to win the bursary.

There were sixteen girls and two boys for the first year at the ballet school. The first year was Elementary, with an examination at the end of the year. Classes always started at the barre, which was a long wooden pole fixed to the wall with dancers doing various exercises to warm up the body.

The second part was in the centre of the room and called adagio, which was slower, using your arms, and then battisement, which was faster, sometimes moving across the room. The teacher could choreograph these movements to the music for the dancers to perform. Penny found the exercises exhausting, but she persisted and began to enjoy herself. Some of the girls appeared to be jealous of her, because she got a highly commended in her exam, while another girl only got a commended.

On Sundays there was a Ballet Club, where pupils learnt different ballets. It started at 2.30 pm and finished at 5 pm. There was a performance held in the local theatre after the first year of their training. The first ballet was Prometheus, followed by L'Arlesienne. Penny was a blue lady in L'Arlesienne, which she enjoyed as it was not danced on pointe.

Finally the great week of performance arrived. On opening night in the wings, while she was waiting to go on stage, a garland was snatched out of Penny's hands in

Prometheus. She was in shock, and refused to go on stage. The principal was furious and she got a ticking off. Life was not fair.

Penny did well in her first examination of Elementary and got good marks. Some mistakes were made on her sheet, and these had to be rectified. There was a teaching class held once a week. The first one was with babies from two and a half years to five. Penny really enjoyed these classes, as it made a change from the strict routine of class.

Penny's second year was a happier one, although she did not like dancing in the theatre. She was given the opportunity to act, and played the mother in "Muckle Moo Meg", which was all in mime. She had to wear a hooped skirt, a wig and older make-up. The only disaster was that she skinned her toes at dress rehearsal, and had to dance with painful feet. She was commended by a drama teacher who was surprised at her good performance.

In the ballet "The Seasons" by Glazunov, Penny danced a snowflake in winter and a poppy in summer. This was the first time she had ever worn a tutu, as all the other costumes were long and flowing.

In her second year she passed her Intermediate exam, and she knew that the following year she had to prepare for her advanced exam, which she was told was one and a half hours long.

In her third year she was in charge of two ballet classes, grades one and two. She really enjoyed herself and was gaining confidence. She knew that she was too tall to become a ballerina, but was hoping to become a dancing teacher.

The last performance in the theatre for the ballet club was "Coppelia", and she was given the part of one of the dolls. She had to be very still, and only react when it was her turn to perform. In the first act she danced the Czardas with the corps de ballet.

In November 1965, Penny was ill with influenza and was feeling sorry for herself. One day the college phoned to say that one of the girls had dropped out of the pantomime, and would Penny like the opportunity to perform in the show. Penny was not too sure about this offer, but her mother persuaded her to accept.

Penny had to go to Perth Theatre in Perthshire for rehearsals. There were six girls and one boy dancer, plus the resident company of actors. The pantomime was "Cinderella." Rehearsals were held in a hall for three weeks, from 10am to sometimes ten at night. It was all very tiring, but Penny started to enjoy stage dancing. Some of the men in the repertory company were not dancers at all and found it hard to do some of the numbers. The choreographer and producer left after the opening night.

In the number "Singing in the Rain", an umbrella which had an elastic tag attached to it got caught on the spokes of the brolly when you tried to put the umbrella up, so Penny cut it off. It was rather embarrassing trying to put an umbrella up when it got stuck.

Penny had another disaster on the opening night, as she did not have time to do up her dress before being called on stage for act two. During the song "Doh a Deer" from the Sound of Music, one of the dancers told Penny that Christopher, one of the actors, had been staring at Penny. Penny had not noticed this before. She found him handsome. He was tall, but he was not a dancer and he found the dance numbers difficult.

Penny never had time for romance; she started paying attention to the male actors. She was placed with Tony for quite a few numbers, but never Christopher. She knew that Christopher was going out with one of the girls from the repertory company and she would give him side glances, hoping he would speak to her.

On Hogmanay her parents travelled up to Perth to see her in the show. It was a cold, snowy evening, and the cast had been invited to the stage manager's house for a party. Penny was dressed in blue with high heels. They all rocked and rolled and jived the evening away. Penny danced with Tony, who was not a bad dancer. Later in the evening, Penny, Jean and Angela were invited to a party given by one of the stage hands. They travelled to various houses and sherry was served to bring in the New Year. It was 5 am when Penny returned to the hotel and fell into bed, hoping she was fit enough for two shows on New Year's Day.

The two shows went well in spite of her pirouettes

moving towards the orchestra pit, and she was glad when it was all over.

Chapter 2

Susan had finished her drama course and qualified with the degree of ARAM, but there were times in her third year when there were rows at home. She and her mother did not see eye to eye and the shouting matches were unbearable. The row was about playing music loudly, because the neighbours would object to the noise. Susan wanted to leave home, so she went down south to London.

Penny's dancing improved, and she was projecting herself well on the stage. She enjoyed modern dancing and tap, but not Highland dancing, as she found it difficult dancing on the balls of her feet. Two sisters taught highland dancing, but if you were not their favourite, or could not manage the steps, they inclined to ignore you.

Penny also had the chance of pas de deux work with some of the boys, but as she was quite tall she towered over them.

One day a lady from Leicester wanted tall dancers for a pantomime held in Brighton. Penny did not have to audition as the woman, Miss Arlene, was pleased with her. The pantomime was "Robin Hood". Soon Penny was packing her case and set off for London for the rehearsals.

The rehearsals were held during the day, and sometimes went well into the evening. There was a lot to learn, especially in the main ballet, which was "Toyland". Penny was playing a milkmaid with another girl, and their costume was lit up with ultra violet lighting. The opening number was a Bossa Nova. Soon Penny settled in and made new friends.

They soon moved down to Brighton, where they met the rest of the company. The show had its Principal, Barry Kent, who sang on the radio in "Friday Nights is Music Night". There was also Roy Castle and children from a local school.

Penny and another girl had difficulty in finding suitable accommodation, and got the afternoon off to look around. They found a place where some of the other dancers stayed as well as the singers. The woman who owned the house had been a trapeze artist but retired. She had a large retriever dog, which usually barked every time someone came to the door.

The pantomime was going well, with three performances on the Saturday, which was extremely exhausting. Some of the girls fell down the stairs, and the producer decided that the five o'clock performance had to be cut out. There was no performance on Christmas Day, which Penny found unusual as in Scotland she had to dance two performances at Christmas and New Year.

Chapter 3

At the New Year party held on stage, the cast enjoyed themselves dancing and trying their hands at limbo dancing. You had to bend backwards underneath a pole and gradually the pole was lowered further. The cast cheered and clapped as you went under the pole, Penny did not do so well, but it was very entertaining.

The pantomime ended and Penny returned to Edinburgh to continue her training. She passed her advanced exam, much to the relief of her parents. Towards the end of that year, she was invited to dance in another pantomime in Cardiff with the same company, "Puss in Boots." This time another girl, called Linda, joined her and both of them made their way down south.

Rehearsals commenced as soon as they arrived. The choreographer, who was Australian, took a dislike to

Penny and another girl, which made it difficult to learn the movements. Penny was hoping that the choreographer would not remain for the rest of the show, as she was a little afraid of her.

The main ballet was "Carmen", and Penny and three other girls were matadors. This was a larger company with leading artists Susan Lane, Barry Kent and Nat Jackley. A local dance school made up a group of children. The girls were not as friendly as the ones in Brighton had been.

To Penny's relief the choreographer left to work on another show and everyone started to relax.

Penny was asked by the producer if she would like to earn extra money, as she knew she was having a tough time trying to find digs in Brighton. Penny accepted and learned that she was to play the back end of a cow! She managed to rehearse with a girl called Gina who had a broad Cockney accent; Gina would be the front end.

The opening number was "Chairs for Sale." One stood on a chair clapping hands before jumping down and turning sideways with the chair. Penny and Gina were helped into their cow costume by a handsome villain called David before performing with the comedian. Gina and Penny had to do a little dance before the comedian pulled Penny backwards so that the cow was sitting on his lap. One time the comedian missed the stool and they all fell on the floor. Of course, the audience were in fits of laughter.

Another production was the "Shoe-Shop Ballet", which

was performed in darkness. The 'shoes' were to be lit up as the singer called out the different kinds of shoes. The performers were dressed in black with veils. First rehearsals were frightening as they were placed on a bench high up above the stage. As the singer called each colour, the person playing that colour raised their costume to show off the shoes. The principal dancer had to step down the staircase kicking her red boots, which was quite dangerous.

One Sunday David arranged a visit to a coal mine in the Rhondda valley. Penny wanted to go as David had arranged it, and she was quite keen on him. They dressed up in white clothing with lights attached to their helmets and proceeded underground, where a man explained how they extracted the coal.

The pantomime season finished towards the end of March. Everyone was glad, as it had become boring doing the same routine every evening. Penny went to London to spend some time with some relatives before returning home.

On her return to Edinburgh she decided to study music and went to her old music teacher, who had retired some time ago.

Penny was advised by her parents that as show business was a very precarious career, she should have another skill such as shorthand and typing. She enrolled in a local school, where she would begin her studies in the autumn.

Chapter 4

A friend from the ballet school got in touch with Penny suggesting that there was a vacancy for a performer on the ballet "Les Sylphides", which would be performed at the Edinburgh Fringe in a church hall. Was she interested? Of course she was; she loved performing on the stage. Rehearsals were in Glasgow, which Penny had to travel through every day. The summer was hot and the sweat rolled off the dancers' backs as they practised.

One of the girls hurt her back and Penny was asked to learn the modern ballet with the music of Gershwin. This ballet was performed on pointe, dressed in a blue leotard, blue shoes. Penny had to learn it in just three days.

She put up one of the dancers at home, as she lived in Glasgow and could not travel backwards and forwards during the show performances.

The next ballet was called "The Servants' Ball", and Penny played one of the housemaids. She was given a solo from "Sleeping Beauty", and danced the role of Violet Fairy. The show had a good write-up in the papers, and everyone enjoyed the week. After all the excitement of the festival, Penny settled down and did her secretarial course. She was asked back to the ballet school to take some classes, and they paid her for her time; this helped her with her studies.

Susan returned after working in London doing various shows as an actress. She suddenly announced that she had become engaged and was soon to be married. She had fallen in love with a chap who worked at the BBC called Frederick Simpson. Her parents were delighted at the news, but Susan stipulated that she did not want a big wedding and requested that a registry wedding would do. After a great fuss, she got married, with close friends and a reception in a hotel in the city. Penny was bridesmaid, with another friend of Susan's. The couple left Edinburgh and went back to London.

Aunt Henrietta saw an advertisement in the paper for singers and dancers for an amateur production of "Summer Song" with music from Dvorak. Penny applied as a dancer. The auditions were held in a hall off Lothian Road, and there were dancers of all shapes and sizes. Penny knew she would be accepted.

The committee sat at her table and a woman stood in front demonstrating a few steps. The tempo was very fast as it was a Hungarian number, so Penny put all her energy into her performance.

The majority of the dancers were accepted, including Penny, and were told that rehearsals would commence in January. For the principals and chorus they would begin in October, but the dancers would later join the company after learning all the numbers.

The hardest dance was Slavonic, which had a fast tempo, and was tricky to perform. The other numbers were the Can-Can with dancers wearing laced-up boots, black fishnet stockings and frilly skirts. Penny enjoyed this number, but it was hard to dance in the boots. The show ran for one week at the Kings Theatre in the month of March. One had to sell as many tickets as one could, and of course her parents and some relatives came to see it.

The following year she auditioned as a singer. This meant she could be on stage for most of the time. To her surprise the music director informed her that she was a second soprano, and was given the book of the show "Orpheus in the Underworld" to look at and study. Once again the rehearsals would start in October for the following year's performance in March.

Susan returned home for a week and told us that she was pregnant. The parents were over the moon about it, telling her to rest. Penny, who always fought with her sister when they were young, was pleased with the news.

The next production was "Orpheus in the Underworld"

and the rehearsals started in October for the chorus to learn all the singing parts. The score was complicated, so it took a while for the voices to blend together. Penny was dancing as well and she had some quick changes, which she managed. There was a woman in the chorus who was determined to be seen and always pushed to the front, even though the producer told her not to. This annoyed Penny and she mentioned to the woman that her place was not there. The woman ignored Penny and insisted in placing herself at the front of the chorus. The producer and choreographer soon fell out, and to Penny's horror the Can-Can dance was reduced to just a twist, and some of the chorus complained that they were not going to wear the masks, as their family would not be able to recognise them. Penny twisted with one of the principals at the footlights and it was all good fun singing and dancing for charity.

Chapter 5

In the third year Penny danced with the company for "The Desert Song", and Penny auditioned for a part in the show. The part was the Arab girl Azuri. Once again she stood in front of the committee, with the choreographer showing her some steps. The music was very fast, and Penny had do twists and turns around the room, as well as having to read for the part. She informed the committee that she was only interested in performing the part of Azuri and was not interested in being an understudy. The part was given to another girl who had performed the part before, but unfortunately she sprained her ankle and had to act and dance hobbling around the stage.

The cast were inclined to be rather cliquey especially the women, probably due to being jealous with some of the dancers and principals. The men were all right and were quite friendly.

Penny was one of the soldiers in the front stage scene, and the principal had to shout when they turned the wrong way. There were other numbers that Penny enjoyed including a modern and tap number.

News came from London that Susan had given birth to a baby boy called Julian. She was coming home to show off the new baby, and of course, Margaret and Matthew were delighted.

Penny was still living at home and working in an insurance office, which was rather boring. She had made some friends, and on Saturday nights went dancing at the Plaza Ballroom. No alcoholic drinks were allowed in the ballroom café, so the girls went to a pub or hotel for a drink or two before making their way to the dancing. The rules were strict, and no one was allowed to rock and roll unless the name of the dance came up on the board. The dance floor was always crowded, and they could only shuffle around the room. Penny had a few dances with several guys, but she only allowed them to see her home if she liked them.

On one occasion when Susan was visiting her parents, she suggested that the dress Penny was wearing was not short enough, and insisted that she would raise the hem of the dress to make it more like a mini dress. At that time an uncle and aunt were visiting, and Uncle George seemed to be delighted that the dress was a mini. Penny at first was horrified that she was going out on a date with a chap called Alec with such a short dress, but Alec did not mind it at all.

After doing the Desert Song with the amateur company, Penny left and went down to London to work. She did some temp work in a few offices before deciding to stay in London. She did not stay with her sister, as they lived some distance out of London, in Surrey. She did manage to rent a small room in Chelsea, and joined a Scottish dancing club where she danced every Monday evening. It was good fun and nobody took the dances seriously. She met a few guys, and went out on dates, but there was nobody she felt she could fall in love with.

One day a stranger joined the class, and Penny fell for him straight away. He was not much of a dancer, but so good looking. All the women were hoping that he would ask them to dance, which he did, as he was rather amused by it all. His name was Justin. He was tall and dark with wavy hair, clean shaven, and had a wicked smile. He did not seem to be married and never brought a partner with him.

Penny found out that he was an engineer and originally came from Wales. He had lived in Wales and Ireland, and was now working in London. He never actually asked any of the women out on a date, but Penny was fascinated by him and she hoped fervently that he would ask her out. She had suggested that after the dancing they should all go to the nearest pub for a drink, so she could get to know him better. Some of the dancers felt it was rather late to be going out drinking, but Penny thought it was a great idea. She was thirsty after all that dancing, and asked Justin to join them, but he refused and Penny wondered if he was married or had a girlfriend.

After a few weeks he decided to join them after all, and Penny loved to listen to all the stories he told them. A few of them left the pub, but Penny stayed on. Although she was usually shy, she told him about herself and what she did in her past.

Some weeks later, Justin asked her to a party, and Penny told him she would accept if it was not too far away. She got herself all dolled up with a new outfit, new shoes and lots of mascara on her lashes. He told her he had a car, and would pick her up at her house. Penny was excited that she had a date, and hoped he would kiss her, unless, of course, he was gay. The very thought of that would be awful for all her romantic ideas.

The party was at Swiss Cottage, and it was in full swing when they arrived. She noticed that Justin kept glancing at her, and wondered if she had overdone the make-up. There was homemade punch, which was rather strong, and Penny nearly choked. Justin poured some lemonade into her glass and told her to drink it slowly. They danced away to the loud music with everyone bumping into each other, as there was not much room. During the slow numbers Justin held her close to him, and she laid her head on his shoulder. He asked if she was all right, as she had staggered a few times thanks to the two glasses of punch she had drunk. She did not want to make a fool of herself, but clung to him as they danced away.

It was one o'clock in the morning when they left the party, and as Justin had not drunk too much punch he had some coffee before leaving. She did not ask him in, in case she landed in bed with him, it was too early for that, so they sat in the car outside her house. He pulled her towards him and kissed her hard on the lips, putting his tongue in her mouth. She was surprised, as nobody had done that before. She pulled away and smiled at him.

"Thank you for a lovely evening, I really enjoyed myself," she said. He looked at her and pulled her against him and kissed her again.

"You are a lovely lass, and I know you like me, so shall we go on another date?" he said.

"Yes that would be very nice" she replied. With that she got out of the car and stood waving as he drove off into the night.

Chapter 6

The romance with Justin did not work out, so Penny returned to Edinburgh where she stayed at home with her parents. Her mother suggested that she should join an amateur company looking for singers and dancers once again.

Auditions were held in a local hotel, and one had to do a singing audition to join the company. It was some years since Penny had danced, except for her Monday evenings in London where she had performed Scottish country dancing. She had some singing lessons from a friend, and found that her voice was much deeper than when she had sung in "The Desert Song". She chose "I could have danced all night" from "My Fair Lady". She sat in the lounge of the hotel for what seemed ages and wondered if she had been forgotten. A large lady told her that the committee were behind in their auditions, but not to worry.

The committee sat or stood near a keyboard, Penny noticed two men and a woman. One was the musical director, then there was the producer, and the woman was the choreographer. Penny felt nervous, and noticed that the pianist found it difficult to read the music and played a lot of wrong notes.

To her surprise she was accepted, and looked forward to rehearsals.

The company was called "Showtime" and all of the performances were taken from different musicals, which made it more interesting. Rehearsals started in August. The opening number was "Another Opening, Another Show" which was a bright number bursting with energy. Penny did not go in for the dancing as she suffered a sore back, but she joined in the big chorus numbers.

The following year Penny decided to audition for the dancing, and was placed in the number "Jesus Christ Superstar". Susan and her husband came up to see the show. Penny noticed that the choreographer, Dorothy Perkins, had taken a dislike to her, ever since she had danced in the chorus in last year's show, and had her mother measure Penny for costumes. Penny knew that she probably danced better than Mrs Perkins' favourites, as the producer had commented positively on her dancing.

After two years, Penny decided to audition for a principal role, and once again she stood before the committee. She auditioned for the part of Evita from the musical

"Argentina", and sang a few lines from the show, but from the look on Mrs Perkins' face, Penny knew she would not be accepted for the part. The musical director's wife always played the main roles. This was not fair, as several times Penny auditioned for a principal role and was always turned down.

Penny made friends with the older ladies in the company. The atmosphere in the dressing room was rather bitchy, as one of the women remarked that she could do much better in the principal roles and Penny agreed with her. Penny told her it was useless going for a part, as the musical director's wife got all the best parts. Penny was also fed up with the backbiting, and decided she had had enough after doing the show for some years.

She noticed in the paper there were auditions for the musical "Carousel" and immediately contacted the secretary. For some unknown reason Penny had missed the main audition, but the secretary told her to come to the first rehearsal. The rehearsals were held in a church hall in Tollcross, and the producer started the company with a few dance steps and songs from the show. Nobody seemed interested in auditioning Penny, as the pianist was not well, so Penny just joined in with the company. She did notice the producer giving her some funny looks.

The producer was a small lady of five feet two inches tall called Judy Gregson. She was well known for amateur plays and musical productions. Penny got a part in the opening scene as one of the women that walked by the carousel, holding a chap's arm. She had the opportunity to sit delicately on a seat, as the carousel moved around the stage.

The number "June is Busting Out All Over" gave Penny an opportunity to dance and at rehearsals, she moved forward to see what the producer was showing them. Judy looked at her and shouted rudely, "Get to the back." Penny glared at her, but did what she was told and moved to the back row. It looked like once again producers and chorographers hated her. The show played for one week at the Kings Theatre, as all the shows did for charity.

Penny went out dancing in one of the dance halls, where she met a handsome chap called Jonathan Williamson. He worked in Edinburgh as a civil engineer; he did not come from Edinburgh but Inverness. He had a good sense of humour and was thirty years of age. He was not like Justin, whom she had thought she was in love with. Jonathan was so different from other men she went out with in that he did not try to maul her or go to bed on their first date. Jonathan was six feet tall, brown hair, blue eyes and a dimple on his chin. Penny's parents were glad that she had found someone, and they approved the relationship. Jonathan's father was a doctor living in Inverness and was retired. He lived in a large house by the river Ness. Penny's mother was a social climber, believing that one had to have a good address and not live in a slum area these days.

Susan had two boys, but rarely came up to Scotland to

visit her parents. She had a nanny to look after them, while she and her husband continued to work at the BBC. Susan worked reading children's' stories over the air, and helping out with scripts for children's' television programmes. Penny never got to see her nephews, except when she was visiting them on holidays and for Christmas.

Penny was had now been dating Jonathan for over four months, which surprised her as all her previous dates were for only three weeks or even a month. She noticed a friend of Jonathan called Peter, who was always looking at her when they all went out together, and she wondered if he fancied her. Peter never asked her out, as he knew that Penny and Jonathan had become very close. Penny asked Jonathan if Peter had a girlfriend, but his reply was that he didn't know. Peter was shy and probably had a girl tucked away somewhere.

Peter Davidson came from Dundee, but lived in Edinburgh, working in a solicitors" office in the West End. He was tall and fair-haired with a beard and loved Scottish country dancing, especially "Strip the Willow", or "Nips of Brandy" as it was sometimes called. This dance could be wild at times, when women were hurled about. Penny felt she had bruises all over her arms when she danced it.

After she and Jonathan had been dating for six months they got engaged, and wondered if they would make their home in Edinburgh or Inverness. Her parents talked about moving to a small flat now that the girls were older. Penny held an engagement party at her parents' house, and Jonathan brought his parents down to meet the family. She invited some friends as well as Peter, but he declined the invitation. He was now going out with a friend of Penny's called Sophie who was a small dark-haired lass and had an interest in musicals and amateur dramatics. She was an outgoing person, who never really stopped talking. The next time Peter saw Penny he gave her a kiss on the lips, congratulating her on her engagement to Jonathan.

Penny and Jonathan got married when she turned thirty, but continued to stay at her parents' home until they found a place of their own. Penny gave up her amateur dancing, and settled down to married life. She would always have these fond memories in her heart.

To Archie,

Fiona McDonald

BVRSH - #0001 - 170322 - C0 - 203/127/14 - PB - 9781861518897 - Matt Lamination